THE GRAVEWATCHER

ROCKWELL SCOTT

Copyright © 2018 by Rockwell Scott

All rights reserved.

No part of this book may be reproduced in any form or by any electronic or mechanical means, including information storage and retrieval systems, without written permission from the author, except for the use of brief quotations in a book review.

THE GRAVEWATCHER

PROLOGUE

It was three o'clock in the morning — the darkest hour of night — and he knew it would come.

That was when it stalked. When it was awake. When it was willing to make its presence known.

Despite this, he remained inside the home, in perhaps the worst possible place — the third floor. The attic was only one room, a simple place for storage. But he had heard the stories. The atrocities that had happened in that room. No wonder a creature such as that stalked the place so late at night.

He could have fled, but he didn't. He could hide, but he would be found.

So instead, he painted.

One last portrait. One final memory. The last thing he would see before it took him.

It would be unfinished. He was out of time.

The painter's brush went rogue, smearing a gash of red where he had not intended. His jittery hand was unstable. So was his heart, palpitating roughly inside his chest.

The rainstorm outside continued to batter down against the roof, the thunder rolling loudly in the distance.

Just as the alarm on his digital watch started to beep, signaling the coming of the witching hour, he heard it.

Footsteps coming from outside. Slowly approaching.

The painter took a step back from his unfinished work, closed his eyes, and took a deep, calming breath. It did little for his sharp, unsteady breaths.

There was nothing left to do but stand and fight. Even though he knew it was a fight he could never win.

There was no winning against something like that.

He dropped his brush to the ground, the red paint staining the floor like blood. And picked up the axe. He'd found the old hatchet when he'd moved into the house, and ever since the strange things started happening, he never slept far from it. Never mind that such a simple weapon would not be effective against the creature that was coming for him.

He turned around and faced the attic door, gripping the weapon in both hands. The painter was an artist turned warrior. He clutched the handle tighter and tighter, knuckles white, his grip slippery with palm sweat.

The footsteps stopped just outside the door.

When it opened, he saw something he didn't expect. A different kind of monster had come calling. But one equally dangerous.

"So," the painter said. "It's come to this."

His visitor said nothing. Probably because there was nothing left to say.

The Gravewatcher

And he knew the end had come. So he raised his weapon and charged, a loud cry bellowing from his lungs as he made his last stand.

Mary Ann looked at her as if she were transforming into a monster before her eyes.

"Cancel the meeting," she squeaked out. "I have to go."

As the sinking feeling in her stomach deepened, Eleanor watched the sun go down over the Manhattan skyline. It was a view she usually enjoyed, but that evening, she was unable to focus on it.

She rubbed the middle of her forehead, eyes closed, and pressed into the headache that had grown.

The heavy feeling that had taken her at the office had grown. She knew it was a strong gut reaction — one that told her the message was true.

Dead.

Dennis. Her youngest brother. That would make him only twenty-eight years old.

Eleanor had never known how strong an intuition could be until then. And, just like any other intuition, she couldn't explain where it came from.

Perhaps her phone acting up when trying to call him.

The device laid on her coffee table, untouched since she'd arrived home, as if she were afraid. It had since returned to working order. The text messages and social media notifications sprouted up.

She had not seen Dennis in four years. There was no mention in the message of what had happened to him, why he had died, or anything else. Not even where to find him. The family was not exactly close anymore, not after their parents had passed away five years ago.

Eleanor slowly realized she had to make a move. She

could not continue to amble about her apartment, lost in sickening dread all night.

Carl.

Her oldest brother was thirty-nine and worked as a lawyer in California. She needed someone to bounce ideas off of, and he seemed the most likely candidate.

She picked up her phone for the first time in hours. It felt heavy. Her hands trembled as she found Carl's name in her contacts. The memories of the blowout fight they'd had the last time they saw each other at their parent's funeral came back unbidden.

Of course, he did not answer. She wanted to hang up, but instead left a message.

"Hey Carl. It's Eleanor. Sorry to bother you, but I received a message today from an anonymous caller about Dennis. Did you get anything similar? Please call me back as soon as you get this."

Next, she called Fred, her other brother. Fred was a cinematographer who worked for a travel show. He spent most of the year out of town, getting flown around the world to film in all kinds of crazy places. There was a time when she'd envied him, but he'd showed up to the funeral looking tired and haggard and displaced. When asked about all the amazing places he'd been and seen, he only shook his head and said it wasn't like that. He was brought in to shoot for five or ten days straight and then would leave immediately. No tourism, no sightseeing, no adventures. Only work and crappy hotel rooms.

Much to her surprise, Fred answered.

"Hey Eleanor." He sounded exhausted.

"Hey Fred. How are you?"

"Good." His heavy breathing crackled the phone line. "You?"

"Good."

Then silence. Eleanor stood, pacing as she tried to think of the next thing to say. It seemed stiff and awkward pleasantries were all the siblings had left.

"Where are you? Are you in the country?"

"No. Down in Nicaragua for a shoot."

A long pause. She felt Fred was just waiting for the phone call to end. He had taken Carl's side in the argument against her. Eleanor had wanted to keep their parent's house in the family. The two of them wanted to sell. It had escalated into a heated, bitter battle.

"Umm. Listen. I got a weird message today. About Dennis."

"About Dennis or from Dennis?" Fred asked.

"About Dennis. He's dead."

No response. All she heard was heavy breathing. And Eleanor got the impression that Fred didn't believe her.

"Who told you that?"

"I don't know."

"What do you mean you don't know?"

"It was an anonymous message."

"So you believe it?"

"Why would someone call and lie about that?" Eleanor asked.

"Because people are crazy."

Eleanor twisted a strand of hair around her finger. She wondered if Fred's reaction confirmed that she was being illogical.

"Have you called Carl?"

Ah yes, just lay it at the feet of the eldest. Fred had the same instinct as her.

"Yes, but he didn't answer."

"So no one told him. Or me. I think someone is just messing with you."

"Yeah, but…" She squeezed the bridge of her nose, trying to find the right words. "I can't explain it, but I feel like it's true."

Fred audibly sighed. "Eleanor, I have a lot going on. I can't do all this with you right now."

"Do all what?" she shot back, voice rising. "Brush off that someone called and said your brother was *dead*."

"But is he? Think, Eleanor!" His anger spiked along with hers. "No one calls about something like that unless it's an anonymous tip to the police. Have you tried calling Dennis?"

"Of course. But his phone isn't working."

"You know how he is. Wait until tomorrow when he charges the damn thing and try again."

"Fred, it isn't like that."

"Look, I have to go. Let me know when you find out he's all right. Then I can say I told you so."

She got the impression he was about to hang up on her. "Do you even know where he was living?"

"Really? Did you even speak to him at the funeral?"

Eleanor groaned. "Can you just tell me, please?"

"Some place called Finnick. A town in southern Louisiana."

"Really? Are you sure? I've never heard of it."

"You've never heard of Louisiana?"

"Of course I have, Fred. I meant Finnick."

"It's apparently super small. That's where he told me he'd moved when we were at the funeral. Can I go now?"

"Fine."

She hung up on him first.

Eleanor collapsed onto the couch. *Finnick.*

She felt the notion forming in the back of her mind. The idea that if she could not get in touch with Dennis, she would fly down there and find him herself.

Fred thought she was crazy, and maybe she was. But that didn't explain the horrible feeling she had deep down.

And even though she was not on good terms with any of her brothers, she knew she had to get to the bottom of it.

As the idea percolated, she flipped through her messages. Lisa, her best girlfriend since high school, was sending her pictures of her new baby. Silvia, a sorority sister from college, had just gotten engaged. Eleanor sent back excited messages of congratulations. Silvia had been wanting to settle down for a while.

There was nothing new on her social media. Mostly notifications from guys she knew in high school and college, commenting on how she still looked good. She ignored them all.

The phone rang in her hands. She frowned. It was James. She'd completely forgotten it was Tuesday, and Tuesday was usually their night.

"Hey," she said when she answered.

"Hey baby," he said.

"Hey," she repeated.

He paused. Then said, "What's wrong?"

"There's been a death in the family."

He was silent for a long time. This was not something they did or talked about. Their relationship wasn't "like that," as Eleanor liked to tell herself.

James was twenty-five — five years younger than her — and she liked it like that. He was naïve, charming, and had a very fit body. Once a week, usually Tuesday, he'd come over and he'd give her the ride of her life, and she to him. After, she gave him fifteen minutes to yammer on about his day before she threw him out. Minimal texts during the week, absolute radio silence on the weekend while he was out hooking up with girls his own age and she was relaxing and catching up on reading, and then back again on Tuesday, ready for more.

Eleanor had given up on the traditional relationship thing — at least for the time being. She did not want a needy man hanging around, always wondering why she was too busy with work to give him more attention, or more sex. She was happy with once a week, and James delivered every time, and was out with other women to satisfy his higher drive while respecting her once a week rule.

She liked him. They'd been seeing each other for six months. And their relationship was definitely not one with an overly large amount of feelings, which is what left him dumbstruck at the moment.

"Don't worry about trying to cheer me up," Eleanor said. "We weren't close."

"So what are you going to do? Do you have to go to a funeral soon?"

"I haven't even heard of the town where he lives. And my brothers are MIA, so apparently it is up to me to handle everything."

"Is that a bad thing?" James asked. "I mean… if my brother died, I wouldn't mind helping out."

"Yes, but you're close with your brother. You see him every weekend."

"Yeah, but still. Family's family. You gotta be there for your family."

She sighed. The last thing she needed was James the boy toy dropping wisdom and making her feel guilty.

"Right. Makes sense."

And it was true. She already knew Carl was not going to get back to her in a timely manner, and Fred didn't even believe her, so therefore it was up to her to figure out what was going on.

And the longer she lingered, the more the feeling that something was terribly wrong nagged at her.

She'd have to go to Finnick and figure out what was going on.

"I'll be out of town for a few days. I'll get in touch with you when I'm back."

"Sure," James said, completely not bothered by the fact that he wasn't going to get any that night. Except he probably was. She knew he had other women he could call.

They hung up and Eleanor pulled her suitcase from her closet, not used since a trip to London with Lisa and Silvia. They still talked about the time Silvia vomited during a Jack the Ripper walking tour. She claimed it was from bad pub food, but she and Lisa knew it was the gruesome details.

She opened her laptop and tried to book a flight to New Orleans, the nearest airport to Finnick, but when she went to click the *purchase* button, her entire laptop shut off.

"What the hell?"

She booted it back up and tried again, but it happened again.

Just like her phone.

Eleanor touched the body of the computer. It was very warm. Almost burning.

And the deep feeling of dread returned. An uncomfortable gnawing in the pit of her stomach.

It was as if some force was trying to keep her away from Finnick. Keep her from contacting her brother.

She had to call the airline to book the flight. It left the next morning. Just as the kind lady at the call center finished her booking and was thanking her for choosing to fly with their airline, Eleanor's phone shut off. The battery signal flashed on the screen, even though it had been mostly charged when she'd begun the call.

As the night wore on, she began to have second thoughts about going to Finnick and poking around. She already knew she was walking into the unknown, but a part of her sincerely believed she was heading toward danger.

3

From LaGuardia to New Orleans, Eleanor sipped dry gin and tonics and accessed the airplane WiFi to look up information about Finnick.

Unsurprisingly, there was not much. It was hardly a tourist destination, with a population of about five thousand. She managed to uncover the name of a local newspaper, but they did not put their issues online.

She searched Dennis Lawson and found no results that matched her brother.

Just how reclusive was he, she wondered.

Did he die alone? Was there anyone there to know he was missing?

She shuddered at the thought. Dennis had grown immensely reclusive, and it had been three years since she had heard anything from him. She'd told herself that she was respecting his privacy, that he wanted it that way.

Eleanor could only hope it was true.

She landed at New Orleans International Airport around one in the afternoon. She rented a car with a navigation system and, having no precise address for her brother, entered in some random location on Finnick's Main Street.

First things first, she thought. *Get to town.*

This was the furthest south she'd ever been, and already it was starkly different from the concrete jungle of New York City. The Interstates were smooth and plain sailing, surrounded by trees the entire way. The leaves were brown in the early autumn, the wind stripping them from branches and blowing them across the road in large bushels. The clouds were grey, although the weather app on her phone reported the chance of rain was low.

The navigation in her car told her to take the next exit toward Finnick. The only sign pointing that way was very small and she would have missed it had the computer not told her.

The ramp off the main highway turned into a bridge a few miles down the road, one that traversed a large bayou with murky standing water pierced by thick-trunked trees. Moss hung from the branches and swayed in the wind.

When the bridge came to an end, it was nothing but two-lane highway straight ahead as far as the eye could see. She passed quaint mom-and-pop stores, restaurants, and trailer parks. Some old man in a pair of overalls waved at her as she drove by. At first she thought he wanted her to stop, but then she realized he was only asking her to slow down — she was still going sixty miles per hour, tearing through the area that she just now realized was a town.

Does he spend his day standing there policing the speed limit? she wondered.

That town ended and the highway opened up again. She checked her navigation. The screen was nothing but a block of green with a white road cut down the middle.

You certainly found your seclusion, Dennis.

The navigation chimed five minutes until her destination. A few seconds later, she passed a sign. All it said was: FINNICK.

Not WELCOME TO FINNICK or YOU ARE NOW ENTERING FINNICK! HAPPY TO SEE YOU!

No charm, no warmth. Eleanor wasn't sure what she was expecting.

The map led her off the main highway and onto a smaller one. It wove through some buildings, the tallest one only two stories high. She spotted the post office and a bank and realized that she was in downtown Finnick. Sure enough, the first street sign she came across read MAIN STREET.

The speed limit down Main Street was fifteen miles per hour. Her car was the only one on the road. There were others parked along the edge — some beat-up pickup trucks, mostly. Only a few people were around. There was an elderly couple walking arm in arm with each other. His body waddled like a duck and it looked like he was covering hardly any distance at all in relation to the effort he was expending. His wife, ever patient, didn't seem to mind. Another was a woman with a double stroller with two young kids. She pushed and walked, and as she did, stared at the screen of her cell phone.

Eleanor slammed on the brakes, narrowly plowing through a game of baseball in the road. The kids — eight of them — had made no effort to move. When the nearest one realized just how close he'd come to getting run over, he only turned and stared at her, as if confused why their game didn't get the right of way.

Why are you just standing there? she wondered. *Get out of the way!*

They were a rag-tag group. Some were tall and lanky, others short and fat, one with a twisted hand from cerebral palsy. Eleanor thought they weren't going to move out of her way, make her go around, but then, slowly, they picked up their balls and bat and slinked to the side of the road. She drove past as their eyes followed her like a room full of portraits.

"You have reached your destination," the car announced. Eleanor pulled over to the side of the road and parked.

If the message had been fake, then she should be able to track down Dennis without much effort. Although he was secluded, he surely had friends, or at least acquaintances. *Someone* in town would know who he was and where to find him.

The random address she had put in the system turned out to be a restaurant called The Flat Tire. It seemed as good a place to start as any.

Do this the old fashioned way, she thought. *Just start asking the locals.*

She got out of the car and approached the parking meter. She dropped two quarters inside, but nothing happened. The thing had been broken and not repaired.

The Flat Tire was an old country bar and restaurant. She'd been in a few like it and had always enjoyed the vibe they were going for. This place, however, wasn't going for a vibe. Instead, it just *was* the old country bar. The inside smelled like the wooden walls. The tables and chairs were mismatched, and each looked uniquely handcrafted. Pool balls clacked together as a large, broad-shouldered man jabbed the cue sharply. A cigarette hung from his mouth. His opponent — a younger guy with a cap drawn low over his eyes watched her as she walked across the restaurant. Faint country music played overhead. A blonde teenage girl deftly maneuvered past Eleanor with a giant tray of food, which she brought to a small family in the corner. The toddler sat in a high chair playing with a toy. The waitress reminded Eleanor of Mary Ann, her assistant.

The bar was quite crowded. There was a row of older gentleman sidled up on stools and staring at television sets mounted above. One played FOX News, the other sports highlights. There were four men in total, all appearing retirement age.

Eleanor took an empty barstool. The surrounding men only spared her a short glance before returning their eyes to the TVs.

The girl behind the bar acknowledged Eleanor, but kept texting on her cell phone. A minute later, after she sent her message, she strolled over. She rested her hand on the counter, pointing her finger at Eleanor.

"Gin and tonic, please."

The girl got to work mixing the drink. As she did, Eleanor was struck by how young she was. There was no way she could be older than about fourteen or fifteen. It couldn't possibly be legal for her to serve alcoholic drinks.

"On second thought," Eleanor said. "How about just a Diet Coke?"

The girl paused just long enough for the annoyance to

cross her face. She dumped the liquid down the sink and drew Diet Coke from the fountain.

The country song on the speaker changed over to one that sounded exactly like the one before.

"Hmm, good tune," muttered one of the drinkers at the end of the bar.

The elderly gentleman next to her glanced her way before turning his eyes back to the television.

"Excuse me," Eleanor said. He still stared at the screen. She tapped his arm. His eyes were wide when he turned to look at her, as if she'd startled him. "Do you know a man named Dennis Lawson?"

The man stared at her blankly for a few seconds, then turned his head around and pointed to a hearing aid in the ear opposite of Eleanor. "Who? Louder."

"Do you know a man named Dennis Lawson?" she repeated, self conscious from her raised voice. It drew the eyes of everyone sitting nearby.

He gave a few minutes' thought before shaking his head. "No ma'am. Sorry." His southern twang was thick and drawn out.

The man sipped his beer and went back to watching television. Or reading the closed captions.

Suddenly, Eleanor noticed a presence behind her. She gasped and jumped, immediately uncomfortable with the nearness of the stranger.

"Sorry, Miss," he said in a deep, southern drawl. "Didn't mean to scare you."

It was one of the guys who'd been playing pool. The one who'd watched her when she'd first arrived. With the hat drawn low over his eyes. It still was. He had a pool stick in his hand.

Without being told, the girl behind the bar drew two beers from the tap — with, what Eleanor noted, a pretty good head — and handed them over to the man.

But he didn't leave.

"Excuse me, ma'am," he said. Eleanor looked over her shoulder. "I heard you shouting at Burt here about Dennis Lawson."

Eleanor straightened. "Yes. Do you know him?" He looked to be Dennis's age. Perhaps they were friends.

The young man furrowed his brow. "Let's have a seat," was all he said.

Eleanor bit her lip. *Why not just a yes or a no?*

Burt noticed the guy. "Oh, hey Sean," he said, voice too loud. "How's your mama?"

The guy smiled back at him. "She's good, Mr. Burt. I'll bring you some of her pie some time soon." Then he looked at Eleanor and motioned for her to follow him.

He handed one of the beers to his friend at the pool table, then led Eleanor to a secluded booth in the back of the bar, a section of the place that she had not noticed before.

Sean removed his cap, revealing brown hair that was trimmed very close to the scalp. His face looked youthful, but probably only because it was clean-shaven. Blue eyes. Broad shoulders and strong arms and chest. He seemed like a good country boy and she wondered what he could possibly be thinking, sticking around in a town like this. In a way, he reminded her of James.

"I'm Sean Benson," he said, extending his hand.

"Eleanor Lawson." She took his hand and gripped it firmly.

"Oh. You must be the sister."

The Gravewatcher

"The older sister, yes." Still, Sean looked confused about something. "So. Do you know my brother?"

Sean looked down at the table where his beer rested between his two hands.

When he didn't say anything, Eleanor said, "Is something wrong?"

"Ma'am," Sean said when he looked up at her. "The way you're asking if I know your brother. Do you know?"

His eyes were soft and wary, and Eleanor suddenly knew the truth.

"Are you asking if I know my brother is dead?" She spoke very slowly, afraid of each word.

And Sean Benson nodded.

Eleanor leaned back in her seat and slumped her shoulders. She stared at the napkin dispenser at the end of the table as if it also dispensed words of encouragement.

"You all right?" Sean finally asked.

Eleanor snapped out of her trance. "Yeah. It's just…"

"You knew, right?"

"Well. I wasn't sure. I got a message at my office telling me that he was dead. But there was no name or number for who had sent it. So I wasn't sure if I believed it or not."

Sean pursed his lips. "Very weird."

Eleanor took in a deep breath and released it quickly. When her parents had passed, she had cried. With Dennis, it was like learning of a long lost second cousin. That was what her brother had become to her in the years since the funeral. Intellectually, she knew she was supposed to be sad, but instead, she just felt numb. "Well. Now I know for sure."

"My condolences," Sean said.

"How did he die?" Eleanor's voice quavered.

Sean shifted in his seat, looking away from her. "Umm." He finally glanced at her from underneath the brim of his cap, as if trying to hide from her gaze. "Suicide."

Eleanor clenched her eyes shut as if the word caused her physical pain. She touched her throat as she processed what Sean had told her.

Dennis. Alone in a small town. Driven to suicide. If we had stayed close, would he have felt the need to do something so drastic?

"I'm sorry, ma'am," Sean said.

"Please. Just Eleanor."

"I hate to be the one to…"

"Were you close to my brother?" she interjected. She felt terrible for putting Sean in the position of having to deliver such news.

"No. I would see him around, though. He'd go to church from time to time. They liked to hang his paintings in the foyer."

"Oh," Eleanor said, perking up. Apparently her brother had taken up art. "Kind of like a local artist thing?"

"Well. I guess you could say that." He sipped his beer. "I tried to ask about his artwork, tried to talk to him, but he was real shy. Kept to himself. Just lived alone in that house by the church. Although he did do a lot to restore the place. Hell of a fixer-upper."

"The house by the church?"

Sean tilted his head. "Yeah. You've never seen his house?"

"We aren't a very close family," Eleanor said.

"Ah. That's too bad. Family is everything, especially

around here. If you don't got your family, who else you got?" He sipped his beer again.

"He was reclusive, as you know. He moved down here years ago and none of us have heard much from him since."

Sean did not respond, and they fell into silence. Finally, Eleanor straightened in her seat. "Well. Looks like I have my work cut out for me." Everything that Dennis owned would have to be boxed up and moved. His house, assuming he owned it, would have to be dealt with. She'd also have to obtain a death certificate.

Still, she found it hard to believe that Dennis was gone so suddenly. Even with their previous estrangement that made it feel like he was gone long before then.

"You need help with anything?" Sean asked, not insincerely.

"Why don't you take me out to his house?" she found herself asking before she really knew what was coming out of her mouth. She caught herself. "That is, if you have the time. And you don't mind. I know you're busy with…" She nodded her head toward the pool table. His big buddy was now playing by himself, sending the balls across the table in a blur.

"Sure, I don't mind," Sean said. He downed the rest of his beer, and Eleanor wondered how many he'd had. His eyes weren't hazy, and he sure looked well enough to drive. "Just glad someone finally came around to take care of his belongings."

Sean rose from the table, but Eleanor stayed seated. "Wait a minute. What do you mean?"

Sean turned back to her and gave her a strange look. "What do I mean by what?"

"You said you were glad someone *finally* came to take care of his belongings. What do you mean by *finally?*"

Sean hesitated before he answered. "Are you serious right now?"

"Completely."

Then Sean said, "Dennis died three months ago."

4

Three months ago.

Eleanor's whole body went rigid. A sudden coldness spread throughout her core.

"You didn't know it was that long ago?" Sean asked.

It was not mentioned in the message that Mary Ann had taken.

Why would the sender leave out the fact that Dennis had died three whole months ago? Probably for the same reason they didn't mention their name.

What the hell was going on?

"Eleanor?"

Eleanor pressed her eyes closed and opened them again, focusing on Sean. "Are you sure? Three whole months?"

"When did you get the message?"

"Two days ago."

Sean adjusted the cap on his head. Up and down, but it settled in the same position over his eyes as it had been before. "That's weird. Dennis died…" His eyes went to the side as he recollected. "Sometime in July?"

It was the end of October.

Eleanor fanned her hand onto her chest, feeling her rapidly beating heart. That new bit of information confirmed that something was very wrong. And she got the feeling it was something she shouldn't meddle in alone.

"Do you know who found him?" Then a horrifying thought struck her. "Do you know how long after he died before he was found?"

Sean shrugged. "Sorry. I don't really know any of this."

"Right," Eleanor said. "Sorry to put this all on you. I'm just…"

"I get it," Sean said. "It is very strange. And sad."

Eleanor took a moment to gather herself.

"Do you still want me to take you out to the house he lived in?" Sean asked.

"Yes, please," Eleanor said. There was a lot to do and even more to discover, but the house seemed to be a good place to start.

Sean owned a silver pickup truck that looked brand new. Eleanor had to leap into the passenger side and grapple with the handrail to keep from tumbling out.

The drive from Main Street took them through small, winding roads. Most didn't have a divider painted down the middle and the narrowness made Eleanor think they were driving down one-way streets. They passed the elementary school, about the size of a convenience store.

The park was open, but no one was there. The PE class at the high school next door was divided into two teams on the front lawn, playing a game of football.

Sean slowed and took a careful turn onto a dirt road. It ran through a copse of trees, all of which were almost bare of their leaves. The crunchy corpses of them settled near the roots, covering the brown grass completely. As they drove, a plume of dust kicked up behind the tires.

The dirt path curved slightly, then the trees ended. The road opened up onto the property.

The house was larger than she expected. Two stories, painted baby blue. It was definitely old, and would be charming to anyone who liked old houses. It sat quiet and alone, out of reach of the rest of the town.

Sean parked the truck and Eleanor got out. The air had taken on more of a chill since they'd left the bar. She pulled her coat around her, crossed her arms, and took a few steps closer to the house.

"One of the oldest houses in Finnick," Sean told her. He stood beside her, hands in his pockets. "Built during the first World War I heard once. No one really wanted the thing for a while until Dennis came to town. It was set to be demolished, but then he fixed her up. Believe me, it looked nothing like this before. He did her a favor."

Eleanor tilted her head to the side. "It's very… quiet."

"Just as he liked it, I guess. Do you want to go inside?"

"Do you have the key?"

Sean shrugged. "No one really locks their doors around here. It's no problem."

"Umm. Okay, sure."

Sean led the way. The front porch was painted black. The wood underneath seemed new, but creaked under their feet. She could see where Dennis had attempted to install a porch swing, but only one side hung from the ceiling of the porch. The other was on the floor.

Sure enough, just as Sean promised, the door opened.

All the curtains had been drawn, blocking out the sun. The air was thick inside, warm and musty and old. It made Eleanor want to gag. The other thing about old houses — they smelled old. And she hated the smell. Give her a new apartment with new amenities in Manhattan any day.

"Let's get some lights on in here," Sean said. He disappeared into a dark room on the left, his thick boots stomping heavily on the wooden floors. He threw the curtains open and light filled the house.

She stood in a foyer. It was a square room that led directly to the staircase in front of them. The stairs wound up against the wall, at first on the right, then twisting to the left before reaching the landing.

She flipped a nearby light switch and was surprised when the bulb overhead flickered to life.

"The power's still on?" she asked.

Sean looked up and scratched his head. "Obviously. But who's paying for it?"

"Does someone live here?" Eleanor asked.

"Nah. I'd have heard about it if someone moved in." Although Sean didn't seem completely sure.

On the left was a living room. Couches, chairs, a fireplace, and a piano, of all things. She didn't think Dennis knew how to play. All the furniture was mismatched and looked as if it had come from consignment stores. Maybe it had.

To the right was a dining room. Unlike the living

room, the table looked brand new and modern, lending even further to the mismatched furniture theme. It was rectangular and made of dark mahogany, and could easily seat eight dinner guests. An unusual choice for Dennis, she thought, but any smaller table wouldn't fit the room.

"All of his stuff is still here," she said when Sean came back into the foyer. "It's like he's gone on vacation instead of…"

"Yes, it is strange," Sean said, looking around. "I guess I just assumed someone was handling it. Now I know y'all didn't even know."

Sean pulled up his jacket sleeve and looked at his watch. "It's getting a bit late." He trailed off.

"Sorry for putting you out," Eleanor said.

"Not at all. Want me to take you back to your car?"

Eleanor had forgotten that she'd left the rental on Main Street. "Sure. Thank you."

Twenty minutes later, Sean pulled up alongside her car, where she'd left it outside the bar. He looked at her. "Look, I know you're in a weird situation. New here, don't really have many answers, and all that. If you need any help or anything, just call me."

"I appreciate that," Eleanor said.

She pulled out her phone and Sean typed his number in. She called him and he saved her number as well.

"You need a hotel or something?" Sean asked.

"Actually," Eleanor said. "I think I'll go back to Dennis's house. Stay there."

Sean raised his eyebrows. "You sure? No one's lived there for months."

"All of his belongings need to be sorted and moved, and the sooner I get started, the better."

Sean seemed put off by the idea.

"What's wrong?" Eleanor asked. "Even the power is still on."

"Yeah, but…" He looked away.

"What?"

He shook his head. "Nothing. You'll think it's crazy."

"Sean. After the day I've had, I'm willing to believe almost anything."

He chuckled, but was still unsure. "There's always been stories about that house." He readjusted his cap.

"Stories?"

"Yeah. You know, like weird stuff that happens. Or things that people have claimed they saw."

"I don't understand," Eleanor said.

"Just some local ghost stories, mostly," Sean said.

"Ah." Eleanor smirked. "Yeah, looks like the perfect place for that kind of stuff. You're right, I'm not going to believe that."

"Yeah…"

Eleanor could tell Sean felt silly for mentioning it, and she wondered if he actually believed what he'd heard. His face had definitely turned a bright shade of red.

"Forget it," he said. "You remember the way back?"

"Finnick isn't too complicated. I got it, I think."

Eleanor got out of the truck and Sean drove away down Main Street.

Although Sean was a stranger, she liked him. He was what she wanted to associate with the small town.

She smiled to herself as she climbed into her rental, still amused that a grown man would still be put off by local urban legends.

5

Eleanor returned to Dennis's house without getting lost. Although it was easy to find, it was still hidden far away from the main road on its isolated dirt path. She parked the car on the grass in front of the house.

Eleanor went back inside and closed the door behind her. The night chill crept in behind her, and she shivered. Once the door was closed, however, the empty house felt very heavy. The silence, the thick air, the strange smell — all of it was stronger when she didn't have Sean there to distract her.

All in all, she felt very unsettled in the place.

She walked throughout the first floor of the house, scoping the place out. As she did, morbid thoughts crept into her mind. Thoughts that she hadn't considered yet, but now that she was alone, ones she could not get out of her head.

Like where, precisely, had Dennis been found? The sofa? The bed?

She returned to the foyer and gazed up the stairway. The house grew darker with each rising step. The old wooden steps creaked under her shoes, echoing off the walls. Such loud sounds gave her pause and made her slow down — it was as if the house wanted to remain hushed, and the footsteps were a disturbance.

She shook her head, pushing the odd feeling from her mind. She lived alone in her apartment — even preferred to live alone — and had never felt like this. It was stupid. She felt like an intruder. Maybe she felt like Dennis would not want her there if he had been alive.

She used the bright flashlight on her phone to find her way in the darkness. The top of the stairway led to a narrow hallway, while the landing overlooked the foyer. The handrail was covered with a thin layer of dust. She avoided touching it.

There were four doors. She tried the closest one and found a bathroom. Simple with ugly blue tile that looked ancient to her modern sensibilities. The bathtub even had feet on the bottom of it. According to her friends' Pinterest pages, those were coming back for some reason that Eleanor could not fathom, but she found them creepy, nonetheless.

The next room was completely empty except for boxes stacked on top of more boxes. There was also some old junk, like an exercise bike, a punching bag, an old television with the cord wrapped around it, and a laptop computer that appeared to be one of the first models ever made.

So random, she thought.

That was the sort of junk she'd eventually have to load into a truck and ship away. Or just toss in the trash.

The third door opened to a simple flight of stairs. It was a narrow passage, maybe only three feet wide. The steps were made of plywood, as well as the walls, and looked to be a hasty addition to the house. She pointed her light up. There was another door at the top of the stairs.

Eleanor took a deep breath and started up the narrow steps, the weak wood bending precariously beneath her feet.

The doorknob was rough metal, and when she turned it, nothing happened.

Locked.

Strange. People in town don't lock their front doors, but they lock their third floor-attics.

The last room unexplored on the landing turned out to be the master bedroom. The king-size four poster bed was against the left wall while a dresser and bookcase aligned the other.

What caught her eye, though, was the easel.

It stood in the center of the room near a window. There was a canvas on it — a finished painting.

Eleanor approached it slowly. The painting was quite good. But it was somber, full of strange colors and a weird subject — a graveyard. Tombstones popped out of the ground. Beyond the graves was a shadowed building with a cross on top.

Another canvas was on the ground near the foot of the easel, propped against the wall and facing away from her. She picked it up and turned it around.

It was the exact same picture of the same graveyard and church, except at nighttime. She looked back and forth between the painting on the easel and the one in her hands, comparing them. They were identical. No gravestone was out of place.

Odd. Although maybe it was an artistic thing — painting the same scene at different times of day.

When she looked out the window, she saw that graveyard for a third time.

The scene in the painting was what Dennis could see straight from his bedroom window. The church was there, an ominous building in the distance. It looked to be as old as the house she was currently in. The backside of the church was facing the house, and behind the church was the graveyard. Rows of grey headstones littered the field, surrounded by trees with no leaves. The area was cordoned off by a metal fence.

Eleanor shivered. Had it been her, there was no way she would buy a house so close to a graveyard, much less make it the view from her bedroom window. Dennis, though, had apparently made that view a source of inspiration for his artwork.

She didn't even know churches still had graveyards conjoined to them. She thought it was an old time tradition that had gone away. Perhaps the church in Finnick was a bit more traditional.

Either way, Eleanor was sure that was the church where Sean used to bump into Dennis.

If that was the case, it was possible she could learn more about Dennis there, and what had driven him to take his own life.

And, perhaps, who had sent her the message that had brought her here.

6

By then, the sun was setting, leaving the sky a pleasant, glowing orange. The birds still chirped in the trees above.

Eleanor strode through the thick grass. The field lay on the outside of clear property lines — it belonged to neither Dennis nor the church, so therefore it had grown tall and long. The dead leaves crunched underneath her feet as she strolled, taking large steps to trample down the growth that had sprung up.

The graveyard came closer and closer and she never took her eyes off of it, as if it were going to disappear or run away. As she neared the trees gave way to field, she saw that the graveyard was much larger than she initially thought. The entire backside of the field was obscured by the trees from Dennis's bedroom window. Now that she was so close, she could see the whole thing sprawling into the distance. It pushed up against another forest thick with trees, and that's where the perimeter of the dead ended.

There was a simple gate blocking off the area. The metal was rusted and jagged and had been erected long ago and not maintained since. Like the surrounding land, she wondered whose job it was to take care of it. Whoever the job belonged to had neglected it for a long time. More than likely, they had died, and were probably buried in that same graveyard, and no one in Finnick had taken the task upon themselves to continue.

The fence was not very high, so Eleanor swung her legs over, careful not to graze her pants on the sharp, jagged barrier. There was not much difference in the maintenance inside the graveyard proper. The grass was still overgrown, and the headstones were covered in grime.

Some headstones were fine, intricate works of art — large stone statues depicting weeping angels. The rest were slabs of wood containing the names of family members and the dates of their life. There were even some family plots. A husband, a wife, and a child were all buried together. Sometimes, the dates of the children's lives indicated that they'd only lived a few years. Such tragedy for a small town.

Eleanor walked among the graves. She could tell that it was an organized affair at one point long ago. The biggest and oldest graves were aligned in neat rows. The newer, small stones seemed to have been crammed in between them, as if someone had been looking for a plot wherever there happened to be room.

She scanned the names, a nervous feeling growing in the pit of her stomach. Sometimes the names were worn, other times they were clear, showing the final resting place of some eighty-year-old woman who had outlived her husband, buried beside her, by fifteen long, lonely years.

A gentle breeze picked up. The brown leaves that remained on the trees rustled above her as she searched the stones. A stronger gust followed, blowing off a new batch of dead leaves that fluttered to the ground like rain. They landed among the graves. One even stuck in her hair, which she had to pick out.

"Good evening."

The voice startled her so much that she gasped and whirled around. She stumbled backwards, almost tripping over the marker for Ellamae Lowe, loving wife and mother. She'd been ninety-six when she'd died.

The man who stood in front of her looked about sixty. He was black, with dark eyes and a trimmed white beard. The hair on his head was gone. He wore a simple black suit that was years old and hung from his body. His left hand clutched the top of a cane, which he leaned on liberally, the ending poking through the soft mud. If it sank any deeper, it might tap on one of the coffins underfoot.

Despite his creepy and sudden appearance, when Eleanor looked at him, she felt more at ease than she ever had since setting foot in town.

"Good evening," she finally remembered to say.

The old man stayed silent. He appraised her with his dark eyes. She wasn't sure, but she thought she saw the hint of a smile on his face, one that seemed to say he already knew so much about her.

"Sorry for intruding," she said. "Is the cemetery closed?"

"Oh, there are no opening and closing hours for this place," he said with a smile that showed straight and white teeth — his youngest and most striking feature. Eleanor considered they were probably fake. "Anyone is free to come here whenever they like, even though they most often do not."

The wind picked up again. Eleanor tucked an active strand of hair behind her ear and crossed her arms. With the setting sun, the chill started to set in further.

"My name is Eleanor Lawson," she said. "I just arrived in town today."

The man's smile did not leave his face, but it did transform into something more sad, more sympathetic. "I assume you have a relation to Dennis Lawson, then."

Eleanor perked up. Finally, someone who seemed to latch onto the name faster than anyone else had. "Yes. Yes I am."

He nodded shortly. "Follow me."

The old man withdrew his cane from the soft mud and started walking among the graves. Eleanor followed close behind, forcing her pace — normally quick and busied in the hurried New York City — to remain slow. The man walked with a limp that made it hard to bend his left knee. Without the help of the cane, he would most likely not be able to get around. Eleanor wondered if it was time for him to use a wheelchair and he was just being too stubborn to admit it.

He brought her to the back of the graveyard where he used his cane to point to a small headstone. Despite it being new, it was already dilapidated. There was a chipped corner and dirt all over the carved name in the front. Regardless, she could still make out the inscription.

DENNIS LAWSON

That was all it said. No dates. No epitaph. Nothing.

"He was born on February twenty-third," Eleanor said.

The old man shrugged. "We didn't know. Harold, down at the hardware store, donated this headstone, by the way. He made it on his own dime and time."

"I heard he died three months ago," Eleanor said.

The old man looked away as he thought about it. "Yes. Sounds about right." His southern accent was thick and if he didn't already talk so slowly, there was a chance Eleanor would not even be able to understand him.

"I didn't know," Eleanor told him. "I just found out the other day. Someone sent a message to my assistant, but didn't leave a name. I came down as quickly as I could."

The old man scratched his chin. "Hmm. Curious."

Eleanor watched him for a moment. "I'm sorry. I did not get your name."

"Oh. How rude of me. My name is Simon Cole." He smiled again and extended his hand. Eleanor took it. His grip was surprisingly strong for a man who could barely walk. "I'm the pastor at the church." He nodded his head toward the other end of the graveyard. "The only church in town. Makes me the only pastor. Makes me responsible for the souls of everyone in Finnick. It's a hefty job." His eyes glistened, and Eleanor knew he was jesting.

"I suppose it does," she said. She couldn't help but smile herself.

"I am sorry for your loss," Simon said. "What was he to you?"

"My younger brother."

"Ah. I figured he was a brother, but could not place if he was younger or older than you."

Eleanor was charmed at the compliment regarding her

age, but chose to ignore it. Another matter had sprouted in her mind. "So, you knew my brother?"

"Yes. Probably better than anyone else in town."

"I met someone else who mentioned that Dennis went to that church. Even donated paintings to it."

"Oh yes. Would you like to see?" Simon Cole seemed so excited about the idea that Eleanor could not turn him down.

"Sure."

Traversing the entire graveyard seemed to be a chore for the old pastor, but regardless, he made it without complaining or losing any breath. They passed through a metal archway that delineated the official entrance of the cemetery. The entrance faced the back of the church, and they went around to the front.

"I was thinking earlier about how I didn't know churches still had graveyards attached," Eleanor said.

"They don't, usually," Simon said. "And this one doesn't either. They are not officially connected. The church was here first, then the graveyard followed when the other one outside of town filled up. This was the largest plot of land, so they used it. It's convenient, I suppose. The funerals always happened here, and then the burial occurs just right outside."

Simon used his cane to open the foyer of the church. Inside was filled with warm, stale air. It smelled of the wooden finish for the pews, the thin, recycled paper of the Bibles and Hymnals, and the old musty carpet that must have been decades old.

Simon left the door open and let the last remaining light of the day flood into the foyer. He did not turn on a light overhead. "I hung his contributions in here," he said.

Sure enough, the walls of the foyer were decorated by many paintings, all mismatched in size, color, and subject matter. Eleanor walked slowly along the wall, viewing them as if she were in an art museum.

There was a painting of a nondescript black man behind the altar, obviously Simon, painted from the point of view of someone sitting in the front pew. There was another of the church building from the outside, the setting sun falling behind it. It was eerily similar to the scene that Eleanor herself had just walked through.

There were more of the graveyard behind the church, painted at different angles. Beside those was a basket a fruit, arguably the most painted thing in the history of the world.

"He was very good," Eleanor said.

"Have you never seen any of his artwork before?" Simon asked.

"No. We were not close. I had not seen or spoken to him in three years." She looked at him. "In fact, I didn't even know he was living here until I asked our other brother."

Simon's smile finally faded and was replaced with a look of genuine sadness. "I am truly sorry to hear that. It should not be that way. God gives us family so that we know we have at least a handful of people in His creation that we can count on."

Eleanor took a deep breath and let the sad, solemn words of the old pastor pass her by. She knew she should have taken them to heart. And who knew — maybe after all this was said and done, maybe then the rest of the siblings could get together and rectify the distance that had formed between them.

She doubted it, though. Since she had stepped off the plane, since her first phone call to Fred and Carl — which he had yet to return — there had been complete silence from them. No questions, no offers of advice or help. She was in this alone.

"It sounds nice in theory." She felt Simon was waiting for a response to his words of wisdom. "But some families just are not like that. My siblings and I do not speak. We haven't spoken since our parents passed away."

"That's a shame," Simon said. "Take it from me, a man whose family died long ago. Without family, the world is a very lonely place."

This time, he did not wait for a response. Instead, he hobbled past her and opened two big double doors on the far side of the foyer. On either side of the door were two plants in identical pots, brown and droopy from neglect and no water.

On the other side of the doors was the sanctuary. This time, Simon turned on the lights as he entered the room. Still, when the large fluorescent bulbs flickered to life after a few arduous seconds, only half of them burned. The rest were out.

Eleanor followed the old man into the sanctuary. The carpet was torn and stained with red. It looked like blood. She hoped it was only communion mishaps. The pews were made of old wood and did not have any cushions. The altar was small and adorned with only a podium that looked as if it had been homemade and an old brown organ. A cross was mounted on the far wall behind the podium. Each row only had five pews in them. Eleanor could imagine church on Sunday morning was not very crowded.

Watching the old man labor around the place made it hard to believe that he led services every week.

"How well did you know my brother?" Eleanor asked his back as he limped away. Her voice echoed off the quiet walls of the church.

At first, she wasn't sure Simon had heard her. He kept talking until he reached the front of the church, near the podium. He looked up at the big cross for a few long moments and then turned back around to look at her.

"I knew him probably better than anyone in town," Simon said. "He moved here and didn't say much. Lived in that old house over on the other side of the graveyard. After a few weeks, he started coming to church. He sat right back there, near where you're standing now." He gestured with his cane to the last pew on the right side row. "Every week, same pew, right in the middle. Most folks who come here have their spot, so that was nothing new. What was new was his face. I knew instantly that he was new in town.

"I still remember that first Sunday. I greeted him simply, as I always do whenever there is a newcomer. I want them to know that they are acknowledged and recognized, but I don't want to scare them away. It's a big thing for someone to start going to church. A major personal decision. I know most new attendees look for any reason at all to run back out the doors.

"So I told him good morning and that he was welcome. Any other conversation was completely up to him. All he said was 'thank you' and then he left. I watched him from the front door as he walked across that field and disappeared into that old house. I didn't see him again until the next Sunday.

"He became a regular. And every week, after the sermon, I did the same thing. I shook his hand, told him good morning and welcome, and waited for him to say more. He didn't. I thought that was fine. All people are looking for different things when they come here. As long as he was here, it didn't matter to me. As long as he had a personal relationship with the Lord, I was fine just being a bystander.

"Then one Sunday… maybe six or seven weeks after his first, he came to me afterward and handed me his painting. It was the one of the church. I told him it was beautiful — and I meant it. He told me he would like to donate it to me and the church, to say thank you for all sermons he'd heard. I think he was feeling bad for never putting anything into the offering plate, but all men and women are at different places in their life. I assumed he was not financially well enough to contribute, or he did not yet trust the Lord enough to provide. Come to find out, he admitted to me that they were going to cut off his power and water for unpaid bills. I put his utilities under my name to help him out."

"Did you know the power is still on?" Eleanor asked.

"Yes. I left it because I figured after he died, someone would come. Time passed, and no one came, and eventually I forgot about it.

"Anyway, I accepted the painting. Then, every few weeks, another one would come. After I'd collected a few, I hung them up on the walls of the foyer. He'd amassed his own little museum in there." Simon chuckled as he remembered the fond memory. "And folks loved them, too. They paid me lots of compliments over those paintings. I was quick to point out that they were done by our

The Gravewatcher

congregation's own Dennis, hoping that maybe these folks would go over to him, tell him what a great artist he was, and then that would stir up some friendships among them. Well, they did go to him and give him the compliments. And he was polite and said thank you, but that was about it. He was not interested in talking about anything else. Only keeping to himself."

"That sounds like Dennis," Eleanor said. She then quickly shut her mouth, not wanting to interrupt the pastor's story. This was the most information she'd heard concerning her brother in a long time. And the way he described his memory was so vivid — Eleanor could almost see her brother sitting on the back pew, quiet and alone and not wanting to disturb.

What were you searching for here? she wondered. She'd never known Dennis to be interested in church.

Simon positioned his cane between his feet and leaned on it with both hands folded on top of each other. His eyes fell to the stained and torn carpet and he blinked several times as he tried to conjure up the next part of his story.

"Then, after about a year of him coming in to the church, he came to me on a personal level. It wasn't a Sunday. It was maybe a Tuesday or a Wednesday. I came out from my office and found him in here, sitting right over there." He pointed to the front pew. "His head was between his legs and he was praying. He hadn't heard me come in, so I stood there and watched him for a long time, not wanting to interrupt his conversation with the Lord. Finally, he looked up at the cross, and then at me." Simon's eyes remained on the ground as he spoke, and Eleanor got the feeling that his pleasant story was about to take a turn.

"We stared at each other for a long time," Simon said. "He had tears in his eyes. I remember that clearly. I could see them glistening all the way from where I stood." He gestured toward the far wall, where his office was.

"I asked him what was wrong. And he told me that he believed his house was possessed."

7

Eleanor blinked. It took her a moment to process what she had just heard, but when she did, her mouth dropped open, ready to inquire, but found no words.

Simon sensed her silence and looked up at her. They watched each other for a few seconds. Simon waited for her to speak.

"I'm sorry. Did you say possessed?"

"Yes ma'am."

"As in like... haunted?" Sean's words from before flicked through her mind.

"Well," Simon said. "Haunted is the colloquial term, I suppose. More of a light-hearted Halloween thing. Possession is a much more... serious affair."

"You mean my brother was superstitious."

"I don't think he was superstitious," Simon said. "I think he was very concerned."

"And... you believed him?"

"Of course I did," Simon said, as if shocked that she'd even asked. "I do take such matters very seriously."

It then occurred to Eleanor that if the man believed in God, then it followed that he also believed in Satan, or devils, or demons, or whatever. Maybe all three.

"So… what happened next?" Eleanor said. She was still stuck on the word *possession* but she did not want to staunch the flow of new information. The old pastor had already plugged more holes in the story of Dennis Lawson than anyone else.

"I sat down next to him on that pew and I asked him to tell me what was going on. And he told me his concerns, and it had been the most I'd heard him speak in a long time.

"He described to me about sounds he heard at night. He'd wake up early in the morning, around three o'clock, hearing footsteps and voices. Sometimes he'd hear screaming. He'd get up and look around and find nothing. He was alone in that house for many miles in every direction, so it didn't make sense to hear all of those things late at night."

"Right…" Eleanor said.

"Eventually, he told me he was beginning to lose sleep. These things frightened him, as they should. So he'd stay awake painting, and then still hear strange presences in his house, walking around downstairs or up above him in his attic."

Eleanor remembered the locked door that led to the third floor.

"I told him that in these times of fear, to pray and keep his Bible close in order to recite Scripture. The Lord is the only thing that can combat the supernatural.

"He told me he did these things, but then he told me in time, he would begin to see figures walking around his house. Shadows that appeared to be of very tall men with indistinguishable features. He would never be able to catch a glimpse of them fully, he said. They would always be disappearing around corners when he entered a room. Or when he saw their feet standing in his peripheral vision, he would look and they would vanish."

"I'm sorry," Eleanor said, finding it difficult to hear more. "But clearly there was something wrong. He was lonely and maybe a little... off." She pointed to her head. "Did you help him in any way besides asking him to pray?"

Simon seemed confused by her question. "What do you mean?"

Figures. Leave it to a pastor to think that prayer was the solution to all problems. Still, she did not want to offend the man, so she chose her words carefully. "What I mean is... obviously the prayer was not completely effective. He went from hearing things to seeing things. Maybe there was someone else who could address these... hallucinations. A doctor, perhaps?"

Simon Cole cocked his head, giving her a funny look. "A doctor? Ma'am, the things that your brother was experiencing could not be healed by any doctor."

"But how do you know that he was telling you the truth? How do you know he wasn't just... suffering from a small case of cabin fever? Maybe he was lonely and just looking for attention in any way he knew how?"

Simon fixed her with a steady gaze. His face hardened. "Of course, ma'am, I never doubted him for a second. Because I have had the exact same experiences as him."

Eleanor stared at the old pastor for a long time as she processed what she'd just heard. Just then, it occurred to her that maybe she was speaking with a crazy person. Perhaps everyone in the entire town was just a little bit… off.

"I'm sorry," Eleanor said. "I'm just trying to get to the bottom of what happened with my brother, and…"

"Ma'am, I'm telling you what happened," Simon said. "I know these things may be outside the realm of your world, but trust me… it is very real. I've experienced it and Dennis did as well."

Eleanor took a deep breath and surrendered. "Fine. What kinds of… things are we talking about?"

Simon seemed to grow very dark. She almost regretted asking him.

"For a long time, I've felt that this church was under attack," Simon said. "I spend a lot of time here, and sometimes I hear noises outside, usually late at night. These sounds are never inside, only outside. It's like banging on the walls, or rattling the windows. Sometimes voices." As he spoke, his voice got very low, as if what he said was a secret only for Eleanor's ears.

"Right," Eleanor said, trying not to sound disinterested.

"This… thing. It never comes inside the church. Oh no. It *can't* come inside the church, I don't think. It's dark and evil, and it does not want to be in the presence of the Lord. So when these things happen, I stay inside here where it's safe and then come out when the sun comes up."

"So what do you think this… thing is?" Eleanor asked.

The Gravewatcher

"Do you think it has anything to do with why my brother died?"

"I think it does." He was not ashamed to admit it.

"So you think my brother was killed by a ghost?" Eleanor found that her patience was running thin with the old pastor, as helpful as he'd been previously.

"Not exactly," he said. "I don't think this *thing* directly killed him. But I think it contributed."

"Do you think he was so scared that he might have... committed suicide?" It was hard for her to bring out the word.

"These are answers I don't have, ma'am," he said. "You wanted me to tell you about Dennis and I's relationship. Well, this is what our relationship was built on. A shared experienced with something... that we could never figure out."

Eleanor narrowed her eyes at the old man. She wondered for the first time if he was yanking her chain, but something about the way he spoke told her that he was completely convinced of his own story. Pastors like him had to be pretty good at reconciling otherworldly things in their mind.

"Did you send me the note? Telling me that my brother had died."

"No ma'am," Simon said. "I did not know who you were until today. Had I known, then I would have come up in person. Dennis was a good man."

"I appreciate you saying so," Eleanor said. She glanced out the window on the side of the church. The sun had gone all the way down. Night had fully set in. "I think I'll be going now. If you remember anything else concerning my brother, please feel free to come and visit. I'm staying in his house." She pointed over her shoulder in that direction.

Simon's eyes widened. "You're staying there? Even after what I told you?"

"Well... yeah."

He shook his head. "I see you are still skeptical."

"I mean... I can't help what I believe, right? You seem like a patient man. You probably understand that."

"I do. But ma'am... this is more than just a matter of faith. This is something that you cannot comprehend."

"Well. Thank you for your concern. You said yourself that the *thing* took some time before Dennis started noticing it, right? A year? I won't be there for that long. So we can hope for the best,"

Without waiting for an answer, Eleanor turned and started walking out of the sanctuary.

"Please. Consider staying the night inside the church," he said. "You'll be safe here. I have a spare mattress and everything."

That was one crazy thought too far for Eleanor. Simon Cole believed so much in what he was telling her that he actually expected her to sleep at the church?

Still, she remembered her manners. "Thank you for the offer. If weird things start happening, you'll be the first one I come to. Just like Dennis." She hoped her words didn't come off as too condescending.

When she left, she closed the church's foyer doors behind her. She felt like she was trapping the old man inside. She'd noticed his strange, longing look as he watched her go. As if he were afraid for her.

There were no lights in the field around the graveyard. Luckily, the moon was full and provided just enough white illumination to help her find her way back across the overgrown patch of land.

As she walked, she glanced to her right at the old cemetery. The gravestones were grey and silver in the moonlight, and the silence that hung over them was thick and heavy.

And in the back of all those dead, her brother lay alone, just as he had lived. Dead and unable to tell her the secrets of his mysterious demise.

8
___

The house was silent and still upon her return. Definitely too quiet. She was always in the habit of having some noise going on in her apartment when she was home, whether it was music on the radio or television sitcom reruns.

But there was no television in the house. There was no radio. There were no forms of entertainment that she could see. Dennis must have spent all of his time painting pictures.

Or doing something else.

She shuddered. Too much empty time was something that she truly feared. She liked being occupied, making herself busy at work, often to the detriment of her health, according to some of her friends.

It had been a long day, so she figured it would be nice to get to bed early. Her eyelids were heavy and her mind was stressed and fatigued. She had been given a lot of information over the last six hours, and she was completely unsure what, if any, could be trusted or believed.

Such an odd place, she thought. Never before had she felt like such a stranger. In some cases, she felt like an intruder.

She climbed the dark staircase and returned to the master bedroom. The bed was made, clean and tidy. She wondered if Dennis had died in the bed. No one had told her specifically where he was found in the house.

But there was no telling. Not in a weird town like Finnick.

Still, there was nowhere else for her to sleep. Except for the old church, she remembered. She peered out the window and saw the dark silhouette of the church in the distance, illuminated only by the moon. There was a single light on inside, a room on the second floor of the old building. She stared at it for a long time, waiting patiently in the silence. Then, a dark shadow passed by the window, slow and wobbly.

Simon Cole.

The old man truly did live there.

Underneath the church was the graveyard. In the night, it took on a whole new look. It actually appeared... sinister.

Her body shivered again. If she had lived in that house, she would have made the other room the master bedroom. Why would Dennis want to sleep in a place that looked out over a graveyard?

Maybe that was just him. Maybe she was too picky.

She returned downstairs to her car and hoisted her luggage from the trunk. She dragged it up the stairs, it being heavier than she remembered. She flipped it onto its side against the wall opposite the bed, and the old wooden floorboards shuddered as it landed. A plume of dust rose into the air around it.

She unzipped it. Her clothes were neat and folded, just as she'd left them. They'd barely shifted during the flight.

It was late, so she didn't feel like unpacking. Instead, she found a pair of pajama pants and a tank top and changed into those. After, she threw back the cover and crawled into the bed, which was surprisingly comfortable.

As tired as she was, she found that once she laid down, her mind began to race. Thoughts of Dennis, thoughts of Sean, and thoughts of the old pastor. All of them kept her brain active and awake. She tossed and turned. Every position was comfortable because of the nice bed, but that wasn't her problem. She was still too focused on the day's events to truly relax.

She did eventually fall asleep. But she was haunted by dreams of Dennis, looking as he had the last time she had seen him at their parent's funeral. In them, they tried to speak, but the only sound she could hear was the garbled static she'd heard when she'd tried to call his phone. She woke, thinking the house was much too quiet at night, and that in itself seemed to be louder than a constant screaming in her ear.

Finally, she opened her eyes and realized she wasn't going to get any sleep that night. She rolled to the bedside table and checked the time on her phone. The light from the screen burned her eyes.

It was 2:58 in the morning.

Too early to do anything productive. But she didn't

want to lie in bed and be bored. Too bad there was no television.

She got up and walked across the room to her suitcase. There was a book or two inside, one of which she'd brought with her from home and another she'd purchased at the airport because it sounded interesting.

The light from the full moon shone through the window. If she positioned herself just right, she would be able to use it to read.

As she passed the window, the old graveyard caught her eye again. She froze and watched it. A grey fog had developed over the night, enveloping the headstones, making them hard to see from the second floor of the old house.

Then, there was movement.

At first, she thought she'd imagined it. Thought it was a trick of the eye, only the fog stirring in the light breeze.

But no. There was movement. Someone was out there.

She pressed her face closer to the glass and squinted. There was a person moving toward the graveyard.

Simon? What is he doing up so early?

But the light in the second-story window of the church was out.

Then, as the figure moved into the full light of the moon, she saw that it could not possibly be the old pastor. It was much too short, and a lot wider. And he walked with a sure step, right toward the graveyard. The figure disappeared into the darkness as it wandered toward the metal archway that marked the entrance to the cemetery, then reappeared on the other side of the fence, moving among the stones.

Then he stopped. Stopped in front of one of the graves.

And stood there.

Eleanor waited and watched for a long time. She expected the person to do something, although she wasn't sure what.

Who visited graves in the middle of the night? And when they did, what did they do?

The person did not lay any flowers. Did not kneel down to pray. Just… stood there.

And the harder she focused on the shadowy figure, the more she thought it looked kind of small. Shorter than the average person.

Maybe…

Is it a kid?

Once the thought occurred to her, the more she became sure that it was a young child who had wandered into the graveyard.

Maybe it was just the local kids misbehaving. Sneaking out of the house late at night and going to scare themselves and each other at the graveyard.

Eleanor glanced around the field. There was no one else. The child was alone.

She looked again to the second floor of the church. The light was definitely out. Simon Cole was asleep.

Eleanor was definitely awake now. This was the last straw. Everything since she'd arrived had been way too strange. Now this — the weirdest thing of all. A kid wandering around in the middle of the night.

She knew she should let it go. Grab her book, get back in bed and just read until dawn. But she also knew there would be no way she could concentrate on what was on those pages.

Besides. Shouldn't that kid be told to get back home before his parents got worried?

She dug her slippers from the bottom of her suitcase and went downstairs.

The night had grown extremely cold. She wrapped her arms around herself, wondering if she should go back up and get her jacket. But she decided to forget about it. She only planned to be outside for a few minutes.

Eleanor went around to the back of the house. The white fog wrapped itself around her ankles and legs. The tall grass of the unkempt field that separated her house and graveyard tickled her ankles and legs through the thin fabric of her pajama pants.

She approached the graveyard. The kid still stood in front of one of the headstones, his back to her. As she neared, she became very aware of the loud crunch of the dead brown leaves underfoot. She expected the kid to turn and look at her at any moment.

But he didn't.

Eleanor was right up to the fence now. The kid should have heard her approach. If he did, then he did not acknowledge her.

Maybe a sleepwalker?

She watched him for a long time. He stood almost completely still in front of a certain gravestone. But his eyes were looking straight ahead. He was not staring at the inscription, but at... something in the distance.

She followed his gaze. There was nothing there except more graves.

Then, she decided to speak. "Hello?"

The kid did not respond. He did not give any indication at all that he had heard her.

Maybe a deaf sleepwalker?

She threw her legs over the metal fence and climbed over. The jagged bars caught the material of her pajamas and she heard the rip from a piece on the back of her thigh. She walked slowly up to the kid, the crunching leaves sounding like firecrackers to her ears.

When she came to stand directly behind him, she said, "Hey. Are you lost?"

Still, the kid did not respond.

So she stayed silent and listened.

That was when she heard that the kid was speaking.

Actually, he was whispering more than speaking. Whispering in a low voice, so low that it was almost imperceptible to hear what he was saying.

When Eleanor tilted her head and really tried to focus, she realized she could not.

The kid was speaking some other language.

The words were totally nonsensical.

Eleanor was no linguist, having only been exposed to Spanish in school and a few others during her European travels in the past. But this language… whatever the kid was saying… didn't sound familiar to her at all.

"Hey," she tried again. Now she was actually starting to worry.

This time, the kid responded. He stopped talking, and then a few seconds later, he turned around. Slowly. Not just his head to look at her, but his whole body. As if his neck was unable to rotate.

What she saw was a child, maybe ten years old. He was

The Gravewatcher

short and very pudgy. He also had the innocent moon face of a child with Down syndrome.

"Hey," Eleanor said, tightening her arms around her body. "What are you doing out here this late?"

She tried to keep her voice light and friendly. In truth, she really had no experience with children, much less ones with special needs. Three years ago, she'd held Carl's newborn for about a minute before she started to cry. Then she gave her back.

Besides, she had decided long ago that she never wanted children of her own. That mothering instinct and desire was not fully present within her.

The kid did not respond. Instead, he only stared at her. Met her eyes, looking slightly up. He seemed to look at her but not entirely see her.

Eleanor truly had no idea what was going on. Could people sleepwalk with their eyes open? Did this have something to do with his condition? She knew less about Down syndrome than she did about children.

"Are you lost? Do you need help?"

As soon as those words were out of her mouth, the kid turned around again. Slowly. Only his feet and knees moved. His head and torso stayed rigid and straight. He put his back to her and faced the gravestone again.

And resumed speaking in the unknown language.

What do I do?

She couldn't leave this kid out here. It was freezing, and he was only wearing shorts and a t-shirt. He was a special child, so she had no idea how independent he was or how functional he was on his own.

She turned toward the church. Should she wake up Simon? Maybe he knew whom the kid belonged to.

Yes. That was the best option. He would know what to do.

She turned back to the kid.

He was staring at her again.

She froze. His face was different. He glowered like an agitated animal that was ready to pounce.

Fear shivered through her stomach and up to her chest. The night was suddenly much colder than it had been before.

"Wait here," she said, her voice now a mild squeak. "I'll get help."

"GO AWAY!"

The outburst from the child was so loud and sudden that Eleanor leapt back, completely startled. The voice was deep and dark, something that could not have possibly come from a boy so young.

Acting instinctively, she turned and ran. She half expected the boy to follow her after being so angry, but he did not. When she looked over her shoulder, she saw that he had not moved from that spot. He only stared at her and watched her go.

So she slowed her running. Her breath heaved, completely shot from being so scared all of a sudden.

How did he make that voice?

It could not have been him.

Did she hear it correctly?

Then, he turned around and resumed looking at the gravestone, just as he had been before.

Eleanor shook her head and looked around, desperate to find anyone who was also seeing this crazy scene laid out before her eyes.

There was no one, of course. She wasn't sure anyone

would even believe her if she told them about it the next day.

So she took her cell phone out of her pocket, opened the camera app, and zoomed in on the kid from where she stood. She snapped several pictures of him standing by the gravestone.

She flipped through the pictures, making sure they were of good quality.

When she looked up, she saw that the boy was in motion again. He walked rigidly, back straight, blank eyes staring straight ahead. He passed through the open archway of the graveyard and wandered through the field.

What should she do? Let him go? Follow him? If she did follow him, would he yell at her again? Or would he attack her?

The boy walked away, not even sparing a glance in her direction. He had to know she was still present. But he seemed to have already forgotten.

So, she decided to follow.

The boy walked slowly, so she did as well. Again, the dead leaves and grass cracked and crunched underfoot, clearly loud enough for the boy to hear since they were not far apart. But he did not turn around to acknowledge her.

He was truly in a world of his own.

He went to the main road and started walking along the shoulder. Eleanor followed.

They traversed a great distance, since Dennis's old house was far off from the main part of town. Eleanor's legs became strained and sore and fatigued from walking on the asphalt in her slippers. The cold night no longer chilled her because of the exertion.

The boy, although squat and fat, seemed to not be winded or tired at all. In fact, he walked as if he was used to making that trek often.

The outlying houses of Finnick soon came into view. They were all dark and quiet. Not a single soul was outside, no one at all to witness the boy taking his midnight stroll. Only Eleanor.

Would anyone even believe her if she told them what she saw?

Maybe not. But then she would show them the photos.

She removed her camera phone from her pocket again. This time, she took a long video of her following the boy. His back was to her, but the moonlight showed enough to easily identify him.

She felt creepy filming him like that. But she felt even more creeped out by his weird activities.

Finally, the boy turned off the main road and made his way through a rundown neighborhood. He walked toward an old doublewide trailer, an oversized, rusted tin can converted into a home.

The boy climbed the wooden steps of the makeshift porch, opened the screen door, and disappeared inside.

No lights came on. No sounds were made. The trailer remained in total silence.

That was as far as Eleanor would go. She could not follow him inside.

She assumed that he lived there with his family. Was it possible they had no idea their son crept out of his bed in the middle of the night to go speak weird languages in the town graveyard?

She was sure they did not. If they did, they would put a stop to it.

Right?

She lifted her phone and took one last picture of the trailer. The destination.

Eleanor was sufficiently curious now, but there was still Dennis. If she had time after handling Dennis's affairs, then she would try to get to the bottom of the new mystery that had fallen into her lap.

9
―――

Eleanor did not sleep the rest of the night. She lay in bed looking at the pictures of the boy on her phone and wondering just what the hell it was that she had witnessed.

A part of her almost believed it was a dream. Maybe *wanted* to believe she had dreamed it.

But she knew the difference between dreams and reality. This was very real.

Morning came and she walked onto the front porch, this time dressed in a warm jacket and a hot cup of coffee. The sun rose beautifully over the trees and chased away the eerie fog from the night before. When she went around back and looked at the graveyard, it almost seemed like a peaceful place rather than the setting of the oddities that had occurred the night before.

The upstairs light of the church was on. As she stared at the window, she saw the shadow of Simon Cole walking around. The old man was up and awake. She considered going to the church and asking him if he knew anything about the boy that crept around the graveyard at night. The boy seemed so meticulous and focused on his little misadventure that Eleanor was sure that it was not the first time he'd done it.

Eleanor went to the graveyard, clutching her coffee mug close to take as much heat from it as she could in the chilly, early morning. She carefully climbed over the rusted fence and went to the spot where the boy had been standing the night before.

CARRIE CARSON
LOVING WIFE AND MOTHER
September 22, 1972 - March 1, 2015

IT MEANT NOTHING TO HER, but the old pastor would probably know who she was.

Eleanor glanced at the church again. The light upstairs was off now.

Leave it, she thought. *There's lots of other stuff to do today.*

She returned inside and washed her coffee mug. As she left the kitchen, she noticed a small door that she had not noticed before. A pantry. She opened it and found it filled with crap. An old mop bucket, some canned food covered in dust, and an ancient-looking vacuum cleaner — an odd piece of equipment for a house that had no carpet.

Eleanor was just about to close the door when she noticed something else. At the back of the pantry was a box. She dragged the box into the the dining room, where she sat down at the table and unfolded the lid.

Inside were more paintings.

Hmm. Maybe Dennis wasn't proud of these.

But the paintings were remarkably better than the ones she had seen in the bedroom and hanging in the church. In fact, they looked as if an entirely different artist had painted them.

She couldn't help but crack a smile. *Dennis. Giving his rejects to the church while keeping the decent ones hidden in a box.*

She shifted through them, examining each one.

Eleanor found a painting of the old house that she was currently residing in. It was clear and detailed and showed a keen eye for depth perception and the shadowing of the trees that were supposed to be further in the distance.

Next was the main street of Finnick at sunset. She had driven down that road the day before when she'd arrived in town, and Dennis had captured it perfectly.

He really was quite good. Why is he hiding this?

Then she found another scene of the graveyard. It was, like the others, painted from the point of view of the bedroom window.

It was a night scene, and the graves looked the same as the painting she'd found upstairs. It almost looked like a copy. But something was different, and at first she couldn't put her finger on it, until she looked closely.

There was an addition to that painting. A person among the gravestones. It was an unclear shape, painted to purposely be obscure and shadowy from the bedroom window.

So Dennis saw him too.

It was not the first time the boy had ventured to the

The Gravewatcher

graveyard in the middle of the night. She imagined her brother awake, sitting by the window, waiting for the boy to show up.

Had he ever tried to talk to him like I did? Or did he just watch?

She shook the boy from her mind. "Bring it back in, Eleanor," she told herself. "There's stuff to do."

The first was to try to talk to her brother, Carl. She had left a voicemail informing him of Dennis's death before she boarded the plane. It was normal for Carl to not answer the phone or respond to texts, but she thought the content of that last message would have inspired him to call back for once in his life.

She tried again. As predicted, the phone rang until the voicemail picked up, so she left another message.

"Hey. It's me again. Eleanor. Your sister. Did you get my last voicemail? I'm trying to tell you that our brother has died. Please call me back. I'm down here in Finnick, Louisiana, trying to sort out all this mess. Please call me back as soon as you get this."

She hung up, knowing there had been an annoyed tone in her voice. Then she used the browser on her phone to find the number for the Vital Records Office.

"How may I help you?" The woman who answered the phone sounded bored and unfriendly.

"I'm looking for a death certificate for my brother."

"Name please."

"Dennis Lawson."

"One moment." Her lines were monotone and practiced. Overused. A keyboard clacked in the background. "Here we are. Lawson, Dennis. Should we print this out and have it ready for you to collect, or should we email it?"

"Email would be great, actually."

Eleanor gave her email address.

"One moment."

Eleanor paced around the living room as the keyboard clicked softly in her earpiece. Then something outside caught her eye.

A car had just rolled up in front of the house. A police cruiser.

10

hat the hell?

Eleanor shifted the curtain aside just enough to peek through. The driver's door opened and out stepped a very large man. His tan officer's uniform clung to his substantial body. The car shifted heavily as soon as he hauled himself out of the seat.

"Okay, ma'am. It's sent," said the woman at the records office.

"Thank you."

Eleanor felt the subsequent buzz of her phone, notifying her that she'd just received an email.

"Is there anything else I can do for you?"

"No. That's all."

"Thank you for calling the Vital Records Office. Have a great day."

Then the line went dead.

The police officer adjusted his pants as he surveyed the house. Then he studied Eleanor's rental car next to his cruiser.

Eleanor slid her cell phone into her pocket and went to the front door of the house. She opened it and went out onto the porch. The chilly air immediately swept over her.

"Good morning," Eleanor offered.

"Morning, ma'am." He actually tipped his wide-brimmed hat to her. "How are you doing today?"

"I'm doing well. A little cold, but that's all right." She folded her arms across her chest. "How about you?"

The sheriff shrugged. "Lovely Fall day."

Eleanor stepped down off the porch and extended her hand. "I'm Eleanor Lawson."

"Sheriff Tony." His large hand enveloped hers. He squeezed it a bit too tightly. His face was lined from age and worry and he sported a thick, brown mustache that obscured his upper lip. His eyes were a clear, light blue.

"My brother was Dennis. He lived here."

"I know," the sheriff said.

"You knew I was in town?"

"Sure did."

"Oh. How?"

"Finnick's a small place. People talk."

Yeah, true. Finnick was a small place, but Eleanor didn't think she'd bumped into too many people who knew who she was or what she was doing in town.

"Not much goes on around here that I don't know about," he added. It sounded like something that would be said in jest, but his serious demeanor threw Eleanor off. It almost sounded like a threat.

She laughed it off anyway. Sheriff Tony did not share her mirth, so she changed the subject. "So, yeah, I'm just in town for a few days to collect all his things and bring them back to New York."

The Gravewatcher

"There's moving people you can call to help with the stuff you want to keep. I can give you the name of a few." His accent was very thick, his words slow and drawled. "Dale and his youngest have a moving business. They'll be happy to help you out. Probably can't get you a discount, because, you know, people don't move here or away from here very often. But tell 'em Sheriff Tony sent you, anyway. They'll be happy to hear that."

"I'll keep that in mind," Eleanor said.

Then Eleanor caught a glimpse of the name tag pinned to his shirt.

Tony Carson.

Sheriff Carson's phone rang on his belt. He retrieved it, squinted at the screen, then said, "Excuse me." He stepped away from her as he took the call.

Eleanor watched him lumber around near his cruiser as he spoke. The man had not yet told her why he had come.

Carson.

Finnick was small, so she was sure that the grave she had seen that morning belonged to someone in the sheriff's family. Given the dates on Carrie Carson's headstone, Eleanor guessed it was his wife.

She remembered the email she had on her own phone. She opened the document and scanned it quickly while the sheriff had his conversation.

And her heart sank.

Cause of Death: Single Gunshot Wound to the Chest.
What?

She read and reread the words dozens of times. She scrolled up to the name and made sure they had sent her the right coroner's report.

She glanced up at the sheriff. He waved his free hand around in the air as he talked animatedly.

Dennis had never fired a gun in his life. In fact, he was vehemently opposed to owning them. She remembered him and Fred getting into a huge debate about gun laws when they'd gathered for their parent's funeral.

That doesn't make much sense. Why would he suddenly own a gun?

Could it be that he borrowed one, knowing what he was going to do with it?

When Tony Carson hung up the phone, he ambled back to her. "Apparently Jimmy down at the bait shop has had another heart attack. They're rushing him down to St. Benedict's now."

"Sorry, Sheriff," Eleanor said, "but I was wondering if you could tell me a little bit about the circumstances regarding my brother's death?"

All at once, Sheriff Carson's entire demeanor shifted. He almost seemed... hostile.

"What do you mean?"

"Well, first of all. Were you the one who called my office to let me know Dennis had died?"

"No, ma'am," Carson said. "We didn't have any information on any family."

The people who just emailed me this death certificate could have put us in touch, she thought.

"I came down here quickly without knowing the full story," Eleanor told him. She was about to tell him what Sean told her about the suicide, but stopped herself at the last second. Instead, she asked, "Sheriff, how did my brother die?"

Without missing a beat, he said, "Suicide."

"Right. But... how?"

Carson narrowed his eyes. "You sure you want to talk about that?"

"It's just that I don't have much information."

"Shot himself," Carson said, as if reporting the news. "They found him in the bedroom."

"Who found him?" Eleanor asked.

The sheriff removed his hat and scratched at his head as he thought. "Hmm. If I remember correctly, I think it was Gretta Washington. She spoke to Dennis sometimes at church. She would even come over here once in a blue moon."

"How do you not remember?" Eleanor asked. "Surely you were called as soon as he was found."

"Sure was," Carson said. He looked upwards as he recalled. "Was about four o'clock in the morning. Big bloody mess on the floor and on the wall."

Eleanor cringed at the gruesome, insensitive details. But she pressed on. "But Dennis has never owned any —"

"If you want more information, I suggest you call the state police," Carson said. "They'd be able to tell you more about what happened."

"But you would have been here," Eleanor said.

"I was. But it was a long time ago now. Shame about it, though. He was a good kid, from what I knew of him, at least. No one knew he was struggling."

"Right..."

Eleanor knew that there was something off about Sheriff Carson. As if there was something he wasn't telling her.

"So why did you come here?"

"Like I said," Carson said. "I heard you were in town and wanted to see how you were getting along."

Eleanor didn't quite believe that either.

"Now. If you'll excuse me. I'm going to head up to St. Benedict's and check on Jimmy." He replaced his hat on top of his head and turned away from her.

As he fell heavily into the driver's seat, Eleanor took a few steps closer. "Sheriff." He looked at her. "There's a boy here in town with Downs syndrome. Do you know who I'm talking about?"

Carson gave her a look. A strange one, considering the innocence of the question she'd just asked. It was almost like a glare. "Walter."

"Sorry?"

"His name is Walter. The only kid in town with Downs. Gretta's boy."

"Gretta. You mean the same lady who found Dennis?"

"Yeah." Carson dragged his heavy legs into the car and closed the door. He started the engine, but then rolled down the window. "Don't be going to bother Gretta, please. She's been having a hard time lately and it wouldn't be good for strangers to go knocking on her door and asking her questions. She was real torn up about Dennis."

Eleanor nodded, and she watched as the police cruiser slowly rolled away and out of sight.

Despite what he'd told her, she knew she absolutely had to talk to Gretta Washington. If she had truly been close to Dennis from church, then she should be able to give her more details.

And now that she knew Dennis, Gretta, and her son Walter were all somehow connected, for the first time she felt like she was finally gaining some traction in discovering the truth.

11

Route 56 looked entirely different in the overcast day than it did in the moonlit night. Still, Eleanor managed to find her way back there.

The trailer park emerged on the left, and Eleanor spotted the doublewide that she'd watched the boy enter the night before. It was painted red and seemed very simple and quiet.

Eleanor pulled off on the side of the road and walked up to the trailer. It was very calm, and she started to think that no one was home. She looked around at the other trailers. Not a single sign of life moved anywhere nearby. A dog started barking suddenly next door, but no owner showed up to shut him up.

She walked up the porch steps and rapped on the screen door, rattling it with her knuckles.

She heard footsteps, then the door opened. On the other side of the screen stood a short, squat black woman.

She gazed through the mesh at Eleanor, not unkindly.

The Gravewatcher

"Hello. My name is Eleanor Lawson. Sorry to disturb you like this."

"Did you say Lawson?" The woman pushed the screen door open and looked Eleanor up and down and then let her eyes linger on her face. "You have his nose."

Eleanor smiled. Rather, Dennis had *her* nose. She'd heard it from their mother her whole life.

"Please, honey. Come in." She waved her hand quickly.

She walked into a kitchen that smelled like dishes that had been left unwashed too long. Sure enough, when Eleanor glanced over, she saw the sink overflowing with grimy plates.

"Don't mind the mess," Gretta said, picking up a yellowed newspaper from the table and relocating it on the counter.

"It's okay," Eleanor said, knowing that visitors or no visitors, this was how the woman lived. Dirt, mud, and filth were caked onto the black and white tiled floor.

To her left was a hallway that opened into a bedroom. There, on the floor, sat the same boy from last night. Walter sat cross-legged on the carpet, playing with toys.

"That's Walter," the woman said, following her gaze. "I heard you were in town."

Eleanor perked up. "Oh. How?" Carson had told her the same thing.

But Gretta had turned her back. "Do you want some coffee?"

"No, thank you," Eleanor said, but Gretta had already busied herself at the sink, filling a pot with water and setting it on the stove.

Eleanor sat at a kitchen table covered in newspapers,

magazines, and unopened mail. A plate with half-eaten food rested on the seat of a nearby chair.

"We were all heartbroken to hear about Dennis's passing," Gretta said. She was a round woman, with a kind face and long, frizzy hair tied back into a ponytail. "Much too young."

"Do you know how my brother died?" Eleanor said quickly.

Gretta stopped what she was doing, momentarily frozen. Then she said, "You don't know?" The woman rigidly turned around to face her.

Eleanor didn't answer. Instead, she stared into the woman's eyes, waiting and expecting an answer. She saw Gretta become quite uncomfortable under her gaze.

"He took his own life," Gretta finally said.

"It's just weird," Eleanor said. "Dennis hated guns. He even refused to shoot targets with our dad down at the range. Why would he suddenly own one?"

Gretta furrowed her brow, but did not respond.

The kettle whistled and Gretta took it off the stove, seeming happy for a distraction. She removed two coffee cups from the plastic bin near the sink, where they were drying after having presumably been washed, although Eleanor had her doubts about their cleanliness.

Gretta took a can of instant coffee from the clutter on the counter and dumped one spoonful into each mug, then filled them with water and stirred. She set the two cups on the table, then brought over some milk and sugar.

"I came here because I wanted to talk to you about what my brother was going through," Eleanor said.

Gretta gripped her cup tightly in both hands. She did

not meet Eleanor's eyes. "Oh, honey. What good is there in talking about such things?"

"For my own peace of mind," Eleanor said.

"Knowing these kinds of details won't give you peace," Gretta said.

"You must have been close with my brother. I heard you were the one to discover what he had done. You went to his house after you hadn't seen him for a while."

"He was not at church that Sunday," Gretta said. "He rarely missed church."

"And you went to check on him and saw that he had committed suicide."

Gretta winced at the word. "Yes."

"Did he ever seem upset? Or lonely? Or depressed?"

"I don't remember," Gretta said. "Honestly. I was in such shock afterwards that it all seems like a blur."

"You don't remember if he was depressed?"

"I don't know if he was depressed."

But Gretta squirmed in her chair as she sipped her coffee. Sheriff Tony Carson was a decent liar, but Gretta Washington needed more practice.

"Did you call my office and tell me that my brother had died?" Eleanor asked.

Gretta gave her a funny look. "No."

"It's just that this whole situation began rather strangely. And I'm trying to put the facts together."

"Maybe it would be best for you to go to the police."

If Gretta wasn't going to be forthcoming, then at least Eleanor could ask her about another piece of the puzzle.

"I couldn't help but notice Walter," Eleanor said.

She laughed and relaxed again. "He's adopted."

"Oh. How wonderful. How old is he?"

"He is eleven."

"Does he go to school?"

"He has a homeschool group that meets in the mornings and afternoons," Gretta said. "He's home for lunch right now."

Eleanor cleared her throat. "Did my brother know Walter?"

Gretta's mirth melted away again.

She really doesn't like talking about Dennis, does she?

"No, I don't think so," Gretta said. "He knew who he was. I tried to get those two to talk whenever I spoke to Dennis at church, but Dennis never seemed interested. Maybe he wasn't one for children. Or maybe special children. Walter has Down syndrome, you know."

Eleanor did know, but acted surprised anyway.

Then Gretta grew confused. "Why do you ask?"

"Because he was around Dennis's house last night."

Gretta choked on her coffee. She set the mug down with a shaky hand and wiped her lips. "I'm sorry, that is quite impossible."

Denying it without asking any other questions?

"I saw him in the graveyard from my bedroom window. He was there at three o'clock in the morning."

"Walter was here last night. He does not get up to mischief like those other boys who wander around late at night without their parents' permission. It was probably one of them."

"I have a video," Eleanor said. She pulled out her phone and placed it in front of Gretta on the table.

Gretta squinted at the video, blinking several times, and though the picture quality wasn't great, Eleanor could tell she recognized Walter.

"No," Gretta finally said. "I'm sorry. That is not him."

Eleanor knew instantly she was covering for him.

"I'm not trying to cause him any trouble," Eleanor said earnestly. "I thought maybe you would like to know where he was last night."

"Walter!" she called.

There were heavy footsteps down the hall, then Walter appeared in the kitchen.

"Come see, sweetie," Gretta said, her kind, motherly tone returning.

Walter approached the table cautiously, eyeing Eleanor.

Gretta put a comforting hand on his shoulder. "Walter, this lady says she knows you. Have you ever met her before?"

He shook his head no.

"Okay, sweetie," Gretta said. She kissed his forehead and ruffled his hair. "You can go back and play now."

Walter ran back to his room.

Gretta turned back to Eleanor. "It was one of the other kids in the neighborhood who you saw. Not my Walter. I've heard quite enough of this." She had gone from a sweet grandmotherly type to a trial witness who refused to speak about the matter further. "I think it's time for you to go."

Gretta rose and waddled over to the door and opened it. She stood aside and waited for Eleanor to leave.

12

With no other choice, Eleanor left the old trailer. The door closed swiftly and loudly behind her, rattling the frame. She walked down the wooden steps of the porch and turned to look back at the trailer. It was silent again. Then the dog next door started barking at her.

No one was willing to help her. No one was going to admit to anything.

It was absolute insanity that Gretta Washington denied that Walter went to the graveyard at night. She surely knew. And if she knew, but didn't care, then why lie about it?

Both she and Sheriff Carson had gotten shifty when she'd brought up Walter. *What do they not want to tell me?*

Tony Carson and Gretta were complete opposites in every way. What secret could they possibly share?

Should she even care? *Just figured she'd want to know her son was out at three o'clock in the morning. If she wants to look the other way, then it has nothing to do with me.*

The Gravewatcher

Right. Walter or no Walter, it didn't change the fact that Dennis was gone and that she had a job to do while in Finnick. She would finish packing up Dennis's belongings — keep some stuff and throw away the rest — and head home as soon as possible.

But as she drove back to Dennis's house, no matter how hard she tried, she could not get the baffling memory of Walter in the graveyard out of her mind.

———

Eleanor spent the rest of the day sorting through Dennis's belongings. The furniture was scarce — only a large dinner table, some chairs, a sofa, a bed, and a few chairs in the living room. Entire rooms in the downstairs part of the house were empty. The kitchen cabinets were devoid of cooking utensils. There were only a few plates, cups, and silverware, and all of them were covered in a fine layer of dust. Most likely, Dennis ate out at restaurants or ordered in.

He didn't have many clothes, either. Just a few pairs of pants, some shirts, and one pair of shoes. His closet was mostly empty.

The thing he had the most of, by far, was artwork. He had many paintings, a few easels, lots of old paintbrushes, and papers upon papers of sketches, most of which were unfinished.

They looked as if he'd been sitting in an old coffee shop on Main Street, finding inspiration in the people who were sitting next to him.

Other sketches were taken from his vantage point in the pew at the back of the church. The scene showed a sparsely attended church service and — clearly — the figure of Simon Cole on the stage, preaching behind the pulpit.

There were more sketches of the graveyard. Some of them showed that he had actually left the bedroom window and gone down there to draw the scene from different angles, and at different times of day.

Dennis did have a fascination with the old graveyard, and Eleanor could not figure out what it was. Still, in all her searches, she did not find another painting or sketch that showed Walter among the graves. It was only just the one.

She worked throughout the evening. Every time she moved something, it kicked up old dust and dirt that agitated her eyes and nose and made her sneeze.

As the sun went down, she turned on the lights and continued. Most of the light bulbs were burned out, but there were still one or two that worked, providing just enough dim, yellow light to see. The house was very old and had been built before the times of widespread electricity. Someone added the light fixtures later, and had done a shoddy job of it. Every now and then, the lights would flicker and buzz. She thought she was very close to losing power, but luckily, she never did.

Around nine in the evening, Eleanor decided to head to bed. She turned off the downstairs lights and went up to the bedroom. She closed the door, changed into pajama pants and a sweatshirt, and lay down in the bed, on her back, and stared up at the ceiling. The truck would come the next day, then she and the driver could load it all up. She wanted to keep the artwork, but the rest she would throw away.

The real problem would be the house. The money from the sale would surely catch her brothers' attentions. Then they would suddenly want to get involved.

She dozed off and her dreams were strange and fitful.

When she awoke a few hours later, she blinked several times, not remembering where she was at first.

Oh yeah. The old house.

She rolled over to the other side of the bed and grabbed her phone. Her heart sank. It was three o'clock in the morning. Again.

She glanced over at the window. There were no curtains, so the bright moonlight shone in liberally. Would Walter be there a second time? Did he make it a habit of coming at that time?

Eleanor rolled over, trying to push the thoughts from her head. What did she care if some kid wandered out in the middle of the night to stare at graves? What did she care if everyone denied it?

She was wide awake, and she knew it. The only thing she could do was read. The thing she had tried to do the night before but had never made it to the suitcase to get the books.

And to get to the books, she knew she had to pass by the window. And when she passed the window, she knew there was no way she was going to be able to *not* look.

Eleanor groaned and threw off the covers. The only way to get the thought out of her head was to give in and take a peek. So she rose and went around the bed, the rough boards creaking under the soles of her feet. She slowly walked up to the window. And sure enough, there he was. Standing in the exact same place as the night before. Probably talking in that language she did not recognize.

She already knew that she wasn't going to go out there again. Not this time. It hadn't worked last time.

"What the hell are you up to?" she whispered to herself. Her breath fogged the glass.

Then, as if he had heard her in the distance, Walter's head spun around.

And looked right at her.

Eleanor gasped and stepped away from the glass. She turned and pressed her back against the wall next to the window. The way he turned around — it was as if he knew to look.

Walter probably knew that Dennis had watched him every night.

Her heart pounded. She knew she shouldn't be afraid, but the boy scared her. There was something off about him.

I can't wait to get out of here tomorrow, she thought. *I can't take another day of this crap.*

When her heart returned to a steady rhythm, she decided to risk another glimpse out the window. She leaned her head over, using one eye to peek through the side of the window. Walter was still staring straight in her direction. Except this time, his entire body was positioned to face her. Exactly right at her.

And then he moved. His hand jabbed out, pointing directly at her. It moved faster than she thought Walter would have been capable of.

She gasped again, backing away from the window. Eleanor moved out of the boy's line of sight, placing her hand over her mouth, breathing hard.

Then she jumped back in bed and brought the covers up to her chin like a scared little girl. Her spot on the sheets was still warm from when she lay there before. She regretted her decision to look out the window.

She may have lain there for an hour. She wasn't sure. Part of her still sensed the presence of Walter outside, but she didn't care. She wouldn't look out that window again. Surely he would have gone home by then.

That's when she heard it.

Squeaking wood.

She gasped and sat up in bed. Then she heard it again. This time it was louder, and definitely coming from downstairs.

Someone was downstairs.

Someone was in the house.

13

"No," she whispered to herself. A chill gripped her heart.

She had locked the door. No one would be able to get in unless they broke in, and she hadn't heard a forced entry.

She drew the covers over her chest, as if they were a shield that could protect her.

Another squeak of the floorboards. That time, it sounded like it was on the stairs. Halfway up the stairs.

Eleanor snatched her phone from the bedside table and dialed 911. When she brought the phone to her ear, all she heard was static and crackling.

No!

The same noise from when she had tried to call Dennis. Her phone grew very warm in her hand, and then it shut off. The battery symbol flashed on the screen.

Eleanor got out of bed. Her own squeaking footsteps sounded like blaring trumpets to her ears in the silence. If she could hear whoever was outside, they could hear her

The Gravewatcher

in the bedroom. They knew exactly which room she was in now. And the door had no lock.

She crept to her suitcase, every step on the floorboards louder than the last.

As she went, she looked out the window again.

Walter was gone.

Was he in the house?

She opened her suitcase and tossed aside the folded clothes and shoes. She rummaged deeply into the contents until she clasped a cold object.

Pepper spray.

She stood upright with the spray ready to go, aimed at the door like a gun. It was the only weapon she had, and she hoped it would be enough.

The only sounds were the involuntary banging of her heart in her chest and her shaky breath, which came out in quick and desperate pants.

She waited, arm raised in defense with the spray can, but no one came. There were no other sounds on the other side of the door.

But whoever was there would not have been able to leave without going back downstairs, and that would have created more noise on the floorboards.

She imagined someone standing halfway up the stairs, completely still, waiting for her to come out of her room so they could pounce. They were involved in an intense standoff, each waiting for the other person to make the first move.

She took one step forward. The floorboard squeaked loudly, as she knew it would. She winced and wished the old house wasn't so noisy. Whoever was out there knew she was moving.

Another step, another creak. Then another.

She was at the bedroom door.

Eleanor gripped the doorknob slowly. The cold metal chilled her palm. She kept the pepper spray raised high, ready to shoot, no matter who was out there.

She took a deep breath and let it out in a slow, ragged exhale.

Then she whirled the door open. Shifted her body to look out into the dark hallway, pepper spray armed and ready.

The hallway was completely dark except for the moonlight that crept in through the windows.

No one was there.

The stairs were empty.

Were they gone?

Because she was sure, without a doubt in her mind, that someone had been inside the house. That was undeniable, and she'd heard the footsteps.

Eleanor crept out onto the upstairs landing, pepper spray still ready, and swept the area. The doors on the second floor were all closed. If someone was hiding inside one of the rooms, she would have heard the door open and close.

She went to the top of the stairs and looked down. Halfway, the staircase turned to the right and led to the first floor, to the foyer near the front door.

All was still.

There was a light switch on the wall near her. She wondered if it was wise to turn on the light, or keep it off, making it harder for the intruder to see her.

Creeping around in the dark seemed silly, so she turned the light on.

The stairway lit up. It revealed nothing.

Eleanor inched down the stairs, one at a time. When she stepped onto the landing, the floor let out a loud squeak, identical to the one she had heard through the bedroom door.

Yes. Someone had been standing in that very spot just a few minutes before.

She went all the way down and into the living room. She turned on the light there.

She turned around and swept through the kitchen. The same story. All was undisturbed. Nothing out of place. No indication that anyone was there, had been there, or had entered.

Now Eleanor felt better. Whoever was there was gone. Or had they even been there at all? She knew what she'd heard.

If she could get her phone working again, she would call the police.

She went back through the kitchen and turned off the lights. Then she went to the living room and did the same.

Then she went to the foot of the stairs, turning off the stairway lights before heading up.

When she did, suddenly there appeared a figure on the middle step, halfway up the staircase.

Eleanor screamed and jumped back. It stood tall, maybe seven feet, and was completely dark, except for the eyes. They shone bright and white.

Eleanor hit the light switch, and the figure disappeared before her eyes.

She stumbled back against the front door, terrified at what she had seen.

The thing had been a shadow. Except it was even

darker than the darkness surrounding it. It had the shape of a person and the edges of its body were blurred.

Like something out of a nightmare.

Eleanor tried to come up with a rational explanation for the hallucination. Grief? Fear?

Whatever that thing was, it was gone. Perhaps it had never been there. A trick of her imagination. Her mind was getting the better of her because she was so paranoid. Eleanor wondered if it would appear again if she turned the lights off.

She had to try, just to prove to herself that it had not been real. So she flipped the switch.

The entity was there again. It was like a living shadow. Something not of this world.

Eleanor quickly turned the light on again. Just as before, it vanished. It did not like the light.

Eleanor's mouth had gone completely dry. She'd gotten a good look at the visitor, but did not know what to make of it.

She remembered what Simon Cole had told her of the house the day before.

Could it be true?

No. That was impossible.

Things like that did not exist.

Then, the lights shut off again — this time by themselves.

And it was right in front of her at the foot of the stairs. So close she could reach out and touch it.

She felt a very powerful, negative energy emanating from the entity, like the gravity in the room had increased and was pushing her down, trying to crush her. It caused pain all throughout her body, especially inside her, like she was being crushed like an insect that had been stomped on.

A dark feeling of dread and despair sprouted inside her. Somehow, she knew that the creature despised her, perhaps even wanted her dead. The force of its presence was so strong she almost felt willing to oblige…

Eleanor broke free from those thoughts and managed to get the lights back on, and again, the shadow vanished.

Eleanor ran to the living room and collapsed on the couch. She drew her knees up to her chest and sat there, shaking, staring at the place the shadow had been.

She did not know how long she stayed there. It had to have been at least an hour. In that time, there were no more sounds. No squeaking floorboards. Nothing.

The heavy feeling in her chest subsided, and then went away. Again, she felt like she was alone.

It did not matter. She knew she had seen it. It was not a dream or a nightmare or a figment of her imagination.

That thing was real.

And she felt its presence.

And it did not like her. She did not know how she knew, but that much was clear.

14

Eleanor spent the rest of the night on the couch with the light on. At some point, she had fallen asleep.

She woke up, lying on the couch, no blanket or anything covering her. Her hand still clutched the can of pepper spray. When she realized she had fallen asleep, she sat up quickly with a gasp.

The house was silent. She was alone. The light over the staircase was still on, but the sun of the early morning shone through the window.

She had made it through the night.

What the hell was that thing?

Had it attacked her? She wasn't sure. That terrible feeling had come from it, that she knew for sure. It had not physically harmed her, but she got the distinct impression that it had wanted to.

That it was evil.

Eleanor went back upstairs and found her bedroom as she had left it — the suitcase with its contents scattered about as she had dug for her pepper spray and the unmade bed with the covers thrown off.

Through the window, she saw the graveyard in the overcast light of the morning.

She remembered Walter the night before. Turning and staring at her. Pointing directly at her. As if he knew the whole time that she had been watching him from the window.

It would have been impossible for him to see her from that far away at night.

Enough.

She remembered what Simon Cole had told her the day before. That Dennis had come to him, claiming the house was possessed.

Is that what Dennis saw?

She was startled by a loud, shrill sound. She jumped and cried out, turning toward the bed where the sound had come from.

A second later, she realized it was her cell phone. At first, she had not recognized the ring.

She walked over to the bedside table where it lay, ringing and buzzing at the same time, creating way too much noise. The display showed her that it was her brother.

Eleanor snatched up the phone and answered it. "Carl."

"Hey Eleanor."

The voice was familiar, even though she had not heard it in a long time. Like the rest of her family, she had not talked to Carl in about three years.

"What the hell took you so long to call back?" She was suddenly very angry. "I've been leaving you voicemails."

"I know. I just got them."

Eleanor wasn't sure if she bought that. As a high-powered lawyer, he was almost certainly glued to his phone at all times of the day. He had probably delegated her message to the bottom of his to-do list.

"Usually when you call it's just to check up or something like that. I had no idea that it was going to be something like..." Eleanor could tell from the tone of his voice that he was actually feeling regretful.

"Well, yeah," Eleanor said.

"Where are you?" Carl asked.

"In Finnick, Louisiana," she said. "I've been here two days."

"Wow." She heard him take a deep breath over the phone. "I'm sorry. I should have listened to my messages sooner. Dennis... I can't believe it."

"Yeah, neither can I," Eleanor said.

"Does Fred know?"

"Yes. I called him the night I found out," she told him.

"Hmm. Strange. I never heard from him."

"He probably knew you wouldn't listen to your voicemails," Eleanor shot back.

Carl did not comment on that. "How did he die?"

Eleanor swallowed a lump in her throat. "He killed himself."

"What?"

"Yeah. According to the death certificate, he was shot in the chest."

"No," Carl said. "That doesn't make any sense. Why would Dennis own a gun? He hated guns."

"That's what I thought, but apparently it happened." Eleanor sat on the edge of the bed and rubbed at her tired, achy eyes. After what she had experienced last night, her brother's motive for suicide was unfortunately starting to make more sense. But she couldn't tell Carl that without sounding insane. "Do you know if he had any problems? Depression or anything like that?"

"No, never," Carl said, certain. "If he developed it later, then it would have been recent. But there was nothing wrong at the funeral, from what I could tell."

Yeah, five whole years ago.

"I'm down here packing up his things in his house. Most of it I'll throw away, but some stuff I'll keep. Like the artwork."

"Anything valuable?"

Eleanor rolled her eyes. "His artwork. Things that he painted."

"Dennis could paint?"

"Apparently. Listen, are you going to give me a hand with all this or not?"

"What do you mean? It sounds like you have everything under control."

She closed her eyes and the living shadow appeared in her memory again, like a lingering mental scar. "Maybe, but it would be nice to know that other people in this family at least give a shit, you know?" Her voice shook.

"Eleanor, don't be like that. You know how my job is. I need some breathing room from it first, and then I can call you back."

This was typical Carl. Whenever serious things outside his expertise needed tending to, he disappeared. He pretended it wasn't a problem until the problem cleaned itself up somehow, usually messily. But then he ignored the mess, so why did he care?

It was the same way when their parents had passed away. He was quite content to remain in California and pay for everything, only showing up just in time for the funeral itself. He figured if he threw money at the situation, then everyone else would handle it.

"Dennis killed himself, Carl," Eleanor said, feeling tears well up in her eyes.

First Dennis.

Then a note that she didn't know who had sent.

Walter and an insidious entity that stalked the house in the darkness.

Now Carl trying to brush it all away. It was getting to be too much.

"Eleanor," he finally said, hearing her choked up voice. "What's really going on?"

She debated telling him for a split second, almost falling into the trap that he had a friendly ear. But she caught herself before she could embarrass herself in front of her brother. "Just what I told you."

"Okay. I'll call you back after I finish up these trial notes for a new client. Will be later this evening."

"Sure, Carl," she said, low and resigned. She knew she would not hear from him again, but had run out of strength to argue.

She went back downstairs, dead set on finishing organizing Dennis's belongings so she could leave town as soon as possible. But before she could start, she heard the sound of tires on the dusty road in front of the house. She pulled the curtain aside from the living room window.

A police vehicle was parked in front of the house. The dust it had kicked up was still settling. The driver's door opened and out stepped the robust Sheriff Carson.

15

"Shit," Eleanor muttered.

What does he want?

Carson stood near his car and looked up at the house, scanning it as if he were appraising it. As he did, he adjusted his pants around his substantial gut, and tucked in the back of his beige uniform shirt that had ridden up his back while he was driving.

Eleanor opened the front door and went out onto the porch.

"Morning, Miss Lawson," he said, making no effort to sound friendly.

Eleanor folded her arms. "What can I do for you, Sheriff?"

"Just came by to see how you were getting along," Carson said. He looked at her from underneath his wide-brimmed sheriff's hat. Eleanor didn't even know they still wore those. They seemed impractical for the job.

"Just fine," Eleanor said. "I'm going to book a truck and I'm going to load my brother's things and leave."

"You going for Dale and his son?"

"No."

Carson's smile faded. "Why don't you and I take a little ride?"

Eleanor shifted her weight from one leg to the other. "Excuse me?"

"Hop in," Carson said. "I got something I want to show you."

Eleanor wasn't sure why, but she felt herself obliging Carson's request. It was probably curiosity more than anything else. "Let me get my purse."

She retrieved it from upstairs, and when she went back down, she went for the passenger side of Carson's cruiser.

"Sorry," he said. "You'll have to ride in the back."

Eleanor gave him a look. "Am I under arrest?"

Carson laughed at that one. "Are you cuffed? No, it's standard policy. No one can ride up front. Trust me, I even have to drive my family around in the back. They feel like criminals, although the kids love it."

Eleanor realized he was serious. Carson opened the back door for her and she slid into the rear of the police cruiser. A black cage all around the windows separated the front of the car from the back, and she would be unable to open the door from the inside.

Carson went around and got in the driver's seat, barely fitting behind the steering wheel. When he dropped his weight heavily into the chair, the entire car lurched to the left. Then they were on their way down the dirt road and onto Route 56.

"How are you finding my town?" he asked once they

were on the highway. He steadily increased the speed until they were going way faster than the speed limit.

My town.

"It's a fine place," Eleanor lied. "Very quaint."

"Ah, I know you hate it," Carson said. "People like you always do."

"What's that supposed to mean?" she asked. The back of his head showed through the bars that caged her in. His heavy, droopy eyes were the only thing she could see in the rearview mirror up front. They looked puffy and large, as if he were having a permanent allergic reaction.

"You know. Big city folks. They come down here, thinking that small towns are 'cute' or 'adorable' but then they get all uppity on us and start causing trouble."

"I'm not causing any trouble," Eleanor said. "And I'm leaving soon."

"Well. That's not what I heard."

At first, Eleanor wasn't sure she'd heard the sheriff correctly. Then she realized. "What have you heard?"

Her mind raced. Had she done anything wrong? Broken the law? No.

"Gretta Washington came in to see me yesterday," Carson said. "Said you've been causing a little bit of trouble for her."

Eleanor couldn't believe what she was hearing. "I went to visit her, that's all. I didn't cause any trouble."

"Gretta was real upset," Carson said. "Said you came in there trying to accuse little Walter of some stuff that is outlandish and not true."

Eleanor ground her teeth hard.

"Walter's a good kid," Carson said. Every so often, he

glanced at her in the rearview mirror and their eyes met. "He isn't going to hurt anybody."

"I'm sure he is good," Eleanor said, despite the thought of him turning and pointing at her from the graveyard the night before.

"Gretta is also a very decent woman," Carson said. "Adopting Walter at her age. And her husband, Albert Washington. He died about twenty years ago. Had a massive heart attack. He's buried in the same cemetery that's out behind your brother's house and the church. Sad time for Finnick."

"I'm sorry to hear that," Eleanor said. She was hoping Carson made a point soon.

"Yeah, so, I'm personally very protective of both Walter and Gretta. They need each other, and they take care of each other. Have one without the other and they would be very unhappy."

"I can see that."

"Gretta is fiercely protective of the boy. She won't stand for anyone doing anything bad to him." Carson paused. "Much less some stranger from out of town."

The police cruiser started gaining speed again. Eleanor could not see the speedometer past Carson's massive frame, but if she had to guess, she would assume they were traveling at least ninety miles per hour. They blew past a speed limit sign that read fifty-five.

"I was not trying to cause Walter any problems." Eleanor checked to make sure her seatbelt was fastened properly. "I just… had some questions."

"And that's the thing," Carson said. "These questions are inappropriate. They do not reflect well of Walter or of his good behavior."

"I know what I saw," Eleanor said, finally losing her temper. "That kid was in the graveyard in the middle of the night. He was standing on the graves talking to someone."

Carson did not say anything for a long time. Did not even look at her in the rearview mirror. He just kept picking up speed as they blew down the highway.

"And where are we going anyway?" Eleanor demanded.

The town of Finnick had long since faded in the background behind them. They were on the open highway, in some sort of no-man's-land where there was only the odd farm or trailer.

"I can't have you coming to my town and bothering my citizens," Carson said. "I knew you were trouble as soon as I saw you, and I knew you would have to be dealt with."

Eleanor's heart sank. *Dealt with?*

"What? Just because I wanted some answers about my brother who died three months ago? And why no one in my family was told until now? And why some kid creeps around the graveyard at night?"

Carson glared at her in the rearview mirror. They stared at each other for a long time. Eleanor started to wonder when he was going to put his eyes back on the road.

The speed started to decrease.

Carson pulled up to a building on the right side of the road with many cars in the parking lot and several huge buses lined up around the side.

He put the car in park and got out of the driver's seat. He walked around the car and opened the back door for her. Eleanor scrambled out, happy to be free, vowing to never get into the back of a police cruiser with him again.

"What are we doing at the bus station?" she demanded.

"I can't have you bothering my town any longer. I want you gone." Carson walked around and got back behind the wheel. He rolled down the passenger side window and spoke to her through it. "Go in there, buy a bus ticket, and take it into the city. From there, you can fly back to wherever you came from."

Eleanor couldn't believe what she was hearing. "Are you being serious right now?"

Carson glared at her. "Serious as a heart attack." He looked at her as if he was a father trying to intimidate his misbehaving child.

"I already told you that I was leaving this evening," she said. "And that I have the truck all booked and ready to go."

Carson shook his head. "That is too late. I want you gone now. And I'm not the only one who does. You've far outstayed your welcome in Finnick."

"No," Eleanor said. "Take me back to my brother's house. I'm going to finish packing and then leave when the truck gets here."

"No can do, ma'am," Carson said. "And I would suggest you not come back. Because if you come back, I'll know about it. And if you do, next time I won't be so nice."

His voice had taken on a menacing tone.

Then he put his foot on the accelerator and tore out of the parking lot, almost running over her toes as he did.

Eleanor stood coughing in the cloud of dust kicked up by by police cruiser tearing out of the lot. She watched it make a U-turn on the road and head back toward Finnick, stranding her there.

16

She could not believe it. She had just been threatened by a police officer. Never in her life did she ever think that would happen to her.

And she was angry. Furious. Her limbs trembled when she thought of his stupid, fat, condescending face looking at her in the rearview mirror. Trying to scare and intimidate her.

She turned and looked at the bus station. It was busier than thought it would be. It must have been a hub along a longer line of stops. She saw people loading up onto a bus and preparing to leave. She imagined herself among them. Leaving town and leaving all her things behind and, most importantly, leaving behind the memory of Dennis.

No. She would not do it.

She would not be intimidated by some bully small-town sheriff. It just was not going to happen.

Eleanor was no stranger to the games people played with their power. There were a select few who thought she did not deserve her position back in Manhattan, and they made that abundantly clear by their actions and ways they tried to undermine her. She'd made it very well known that she was there to stay, both by delivering quality work and by not bending to the will of bullies.

And the same would happen here and now.

She took out her phone and called the only friend she had in Finnick.

"Hey," Sean said.

"Hey, Sean. I have a little problem."

She told him where she was, but not how she had gotten there. She just said she was stranded and needed a lift back to town. She tried to keep the concerned edge from her voice, but Sean picked up on it.

"I'll be right there," he said.

It took thirty minutes before his pickup truck pulled into the parking lot. Eleanor climbed into the front seat and they headed back to town.

"Are you okay?" Sean asked.

She told him the story. She watched his face as he drove, listening, and she saw the look of concern cross his eyes.

When she was done, Sean shook his head. "Tony Carson. I always knew there was something about the man. I never messed around with him, even when I was a kid, and still don't mess around with him now. If I stay out of his business, he'll stay out of mine."

"Well, I guess he's decided I'm in his business," Eleanor said.

She chewed on her finger as she stared out the window. The flat, green landscape passed by in a whir. Sean drove a lot slower and safer than Carson. "Do you think he would hurt me? Like, really hurt me?"

"I would like to think not," Sean said.

Eleanor continued to stare out the window as they drove along. Sean fell silent, and she wondered just how much further she should involve him. If he got too close to her, then Carson could come after him as well. Sean may have already come to that conclusion and resigned to keep away from her after this. He'd already told her he didn't want to be on Carson's radar.

"Sean," she said.

"Yeah?"

She wasn't sure why she was asking. But she needed to. Needed to know. Needed to hear something. "That house my brother lived in."

"Yeah?"

"Well. Last night. I had a weird experience."

Sean didn't say anything for a long time. She wondered if he knew where the conversation was heading.

"Okay."

"Yeah. I was hearing noises. I woke up and checked the house, but no one was there. But then…"

She told him about the shadow entity that had appeared on the steps and disappeared whenever she turned on the light. And how it moved close to her and made her depressed and uncomfortable. And the overwhelming feeling that the thing despised her. She looked over at him. "You think I'm crazy, don't you?"

"No, no, no," he said quickly. He adjusted the cap on his head. "Not at all. In fact… you're not the first person to say things like that about the house."

"Really? Did my brother ever mention anything about it?"

"Not to me. But other people around town have had plenty to say about the house. That it was haunted, or that bad things happened there a long time ago. You know, like small town urban legends and ghost stories. Stuff the kids tell around the campfire to scare each other."

Eleanor remembered Dennis had confided in Simon Cole that the house was haunted. Simon Cole had even believed him, and had tried to warn Eleanor about staying there.

"I'm starting to think I'm crazy," she said. "I don't believe in any of that crap. But I know what I saw."

"I believe you," Sean said, his voice low and distant.

"I mean… It was right there in front of me on the stairs. When I close my eyes, I can see it so clearly." She tried to push the image from her brain. "Do you believe in stuff like that? Like ghosts and the supernatural?"

"Hmm. I consider myself a good Christian man," he said. "It's not good for my mind and thoughts to linger on things like that." He adjusted his cap again. "It's evil, all of it. And I don't want any part of it in my life. Because I heard that once it becomes part of you, it never leaves you alone."

A shiver ran up Eleanor's spine. She certainly hoped that wasn't true.

"I have something for you," Sean said suddenly. He popped open the console of the armrest and rummaged around. He pulled out a necklace with a wooden cross dangling from the end of it. "Here."

Eleanor took it, letting it hang in front of her eyes. The cross swayed with the bumpy motion of the truck. She had never cared much for jewelry, religious or otherwise.

"It's nice. I don't want to take it after all you've done for me."

"Nah," Sean said. "I make them. Little side hobby. I got a whole bunch at home."

"Oh." Eleanor felt much more endeared toward the gift. She placed it around her neck and let the cross hang underneath her shirt.

"Maybe it'll… you know. Protect you. Or make you feel safe. If you need it. Something like that."

So he does believe in this stuff, she realized.

She didn't necessarily believe that wearing it would protect her from anything, but Sean had been so serious when he'd given it to her that obviously he felt it would.

And who knew? At that point, she was desperate enough to try anything.

17

"You sure you want to stay here tonight?" Sean asked when he dropped her off. "I got plenty of space back at my house."

Eleanor caught sight of the old church in the distance. She remembered what Simon Cole had told her about the house the first time she had spoken to him.

"I'll give you a call," Eleanor said. "There's something I want to do first."

"If you say so," Sean said. "But please. Don't stay here."

After he left, Eleanor crossed the overgrown field to the church. The room upstairs was dark, and she wondered if Simon Cole was out.

She entered through the foyer door and then went into the sanctuary. The room was dark, barely lit by the light of the setting sun coming in through the windows on the side. The crucified Jesus statue at the back of the room loomed heavy in shadow and seemed to overpower her presence in the room. In a way, it almost made her feel unwelcome.

"Hello?" she called out. No answer.

She walked to the side of the sanctuary and found a small set of stairs that led up to the second floor.

She took them up, each one creaking along the way.

The second floor of the church was more like a loft than a proper second floor. She had to tilt her head to keep from scraping her scalp across the low ceiling. It was almost completely dark, as the windows were too small to let in much sunlight.

There was only one room up there, and it was at the end of the hallway. At first, Eleanor thought it was a storage room, but as she looked closer, she realized that someone had made it home. There was a mattress pushed into the corner, without a frame, and a single thick bedspread, wrinkled and kicked to the foot of the bed. Both were discolored and gross from years of use. A table nearby was stacked with books and newspapers. It looked like someone had meant to recycle them long ago, but had never gotten around to it. Clothes were strewn about, jeans and shirts and underwear and socks, all over the floor. The room had a subtle stench to it, one that smelled of old furniture, stale air, and body odor.

Crosses hung on the walls, some of which were crucifixes. There were pictures of Jesus as well, each portraying him as the white, long-haired, gentle Jesus. One even showed him cradling a lamb on his lap. There were some other crosses on the walls that did not look like the Christian one, but rather some sort of strange religious iconography that Eleanor did not know.

The room had a single window that looked over the graveyard below the church and, in the distance, Dennis's house. This was the room she had seen lit up at night.

This was the room where she had seen shadows pass by the window.

Near the window was a small table that had a notebook with messily written scrawl. It was a list of dates and times. The dates were consecutive, one after another, without a single one missed. The times ranged from 2:58 in the morning to 3:06 in the morning. Eleanor turned the pages backwards; the log went back months.

"What are you doing here?"

The voice behind her startled her, causing her to shoot up and whirl around.

Simon Cole stood in the doorway behind her. The setting sun was not providing much light from the tiny window anymore, so he was mostly in shadow, his dark skin blending in.

"I'm sorry," she said. "I didn't mean to intrude."

"And I did not mean to frighten you." The old pastor hobbled over to another small table near his bed. The walking cane clicked on the ground as he leaned heavily on it. He bent down and lit an oil lamp that illuminated the room.

Simon Cole's eyes went to the notebook on the table beside the window. "You must be wondering what that is," he said.

"No. I'm not," Eleanor said. "Because I already know."

Simon nodded slowly. "I see. What is it that you think you know?"

"You're watching Walter," she said quietly. "He comes to the graveyard every night at the same time."

"Do you often stay awake until three o'clock in the morning?"

"I saw him the first night I was here," Eleanor said.

Then a thought occurred to her. "And if you're watching him as much as you seem to be, then that means you saw me go outside and talk to him."

"Mmm." Simon nodded slowly again. "I did. I have tried to interfere with the boy's habits. It is useless."

"My brother also knew that he visited in the middle of the night," Eleanor said. "He has a painting of the graveyard that shows Walter in it."

"Your brother was very distressed about the comings and goings of the boy," Simon said. "In fact, he saw him before I did. I think he used to stay up late into the night working on his art. That was when he noticed. Then he came to me and asked me about it. Naturally, I had no idea. That is until I started staying up to watch. Now, it has become a bit of an obsession." He took a deep breath and sighed. "I've tried to ask his mother about it, but she'll hear none of it."

"Yeah, I tried to have that same conversation with Gretta," Eleanor said. "What is he doing down there? The grave he stands in front of is for someone named Carrie Carson. Is that Sheriff Carson's wife?"

"Yes," Simon said. "She died about two years ago and is buried there."

"I don't understand," said Eleanor. "Why that grave?"

"I don't know," Simon said. "I have tried before to interfere with the boy and his wandering. At first, I thought it was sleepwalking, and that he was in danger by being out of bed and wandering around town so late. I had no such luck. Then, soon after, I had a visit from the sheriff. He told me to stop 'terrorizing' Walter, and to leave him alone, and that I scared the poor boy. I don't think any of that is true, but the way Carson said it… I could tell it was a threat, not just friendly advice."

"The same thing happened to me," Eleanor said. "He threatened me, told me I was bothering the town, and that I should get out, and that if he caught me back in Finnick, there would be problems."

Simon Cole was less surprised about the threat than Sean had been. Probably because he had experienced the same thing.

"Do you think Carson said the same thing to my brother?" she asked. "Do you think he threatened Dennis?

"I don't know," Simon said. "If he did, Dennis never mentioned it to me."

Eleanor watched the man. He looked truly old and weary and tired as he stood there, leaning a bit too heavily on his cane.

"Simon," Eleanor said. "You told me when I got here that my brother came to you because he was concerned about certain… things that were going on in the house. As if it were haunted or something."

Simon nodded again.

"Well. Last night. I had an experience that I cannot explain."

"I can explain it," Simon said. "You saw that same monster your brother saw. I offered to let you stay in the church, but you declined."

"Yes. But you must understand, I don't believe in stuff like that."

"Do you now?"

Eleanor did not respond. Did not want to admit that she did. She fingered the cross necklace that Sean had given her.

"You still don't know? Even after you saw it?" He seemed incredulous. "Let me guess. It was a shadow. A tall shadow, maybe seven or eight feet. It had small and bright eyes. It does not like the light."

Eleanor's mouth fell open. "Yes. That's exactly it. Whenever I turned on the light, it would disappear."

"Yes," Simon said, his voice low and deep. "You have seen the same creature as your brother."

"What is it?"

"It is a demonic entity — something truly evil. Your brother reached out to me for help. Although I've heard from other pastors who have done battle with the spiritual, it has never come up in my career. I didn't know what to do. But one of my flock was in trouble and asking for help, so I was obligated to lend a hand. I went over there and tried to bless the house, but the entity did not like it. It became very active and violent. I remember…" Simon's eyes went blank as he recalled the event. Fear spread over his face. "I remember being lifted off the floor, as if two giant hands had grabbed me under the arms. Then I was thrown backwards and landed against the wall. I fell on my side and I shattered my hip. I was in the hospital for months after the surgery."

Eleanor looked at his right leg, bent and twisted and barely useable.

"Yes," he said. "That *thing* is what did this to me."

"I'm sorry," said Eleanor. "No wonder you believe."

"I don't just believe," Simon said. "I know. Now you see why I begged you to stay in the church. By the time I got out of the hospital and returned to the church, your brother was dead."

"Do you think that thing is what drove him to… do what he did?" Eleanor remembered the complete and utter despair the thing had made her feel just by being in its presence for a few seconds.

"I believe it with all my heart," Simon said. He looked down at the ground. "I told your brother to flee, but he insisted he had nowhere else to go. So I thought I could fight it for him. Just pray it away and everything would be better. But I was wrong. I was not strong enough. I did not have faith enough." He looked back up at Eleanor. "And for that, I am truly sorry."

Eleanor stepped across the room and got very close to Simon. "It is not your fault."

"I blame myself completely."

"Please don't," she said, feeling very sorry for the old pastor. "I thank you for trying to help my brother. I really do. And now I want to help him too. I want to get to the bottom of this."

"I will do whatever I can for you," Simon said. "But remember… I am just a frail old man and washed up pastor. Other than that… I will lend you whatever services I can."

"Please don't say that about yourself," Eleanor said. She reached out and straightened a wrinkle on the shoulder of Simon's shirt. "You were a friend to my brother. That was the one thing he needed in his life toward the end, I think. You did better than me. I was his family, and I should have been there for him."

"It is never too late to make amends," Simon said. "For both you and I."

Eleanor smiled at that. He was right. She had made the

right decision to stay in town and fight for her brother, to not let Tony Carson scare her away.

"Do you know where that thing came from?" Eleanor asked. "If we know where it originated, we might know how to get rid of it."

"It is an agent of darkness," said Simon. "That much I know. It does not like me, and it cannot come inside the church. It is a demonic entity, and those types of spirits typically come around areas where horrible and tragic things have happened in the past."

Eleanor remembered that Sean had heard stories regarding the house.

"That house," Simon said. "It is the oldest in town. It was here before Finnick ever was. I did some reading before, and it turned out that it belonged to a small African American family back in the 1920s. See, back then, racial tensions were high, and the white folks around did not take too kindly to them. I don't know the events that caused it. Maybe there were none, which makes it all the more tragic and scary. But a group of whites kicked in the door and murdered the entire family with an axe. The man, his wife, and their young son. The story goes that they knew the mob was coming and locked themselves in the third floor attic. When the mob broke down the door and searched the house, it looked like no one was home, but they quickly located the family upstairs. That was where the murders were said to have taken place."

Eleanor remembered the third floor attic she had found her first day in the house. The door had been locked, and she had not tried to open it again after that. Nor had she given it much thought.

"That's terrible," she said, her voice low. "I can't believe that happened."

Simon Cole nodded. "These small towns all have a history. Not all of it is as clean as we would like it to be."

"So you think my brother was seeing the entity that this tragedy attracted?" Eleanor asked.

"Yes. On top of that, he was concerning himself with Walter and his nightly visits to the graveyard."

"Do you think Walter and the entity are somehow connected?" Eleanor asked. "Because last night, I saw him through the window again. He then... turned around and pointed to me, as if he knew I was there the whole time, watching him. It was after that when I started hearing noises in the house. At first I thought it was Walter who had come inside, but then I saw the shadow."

A very dark look came over Simon Cole's face. He looked truly afraid. "Yes, I do think the two are connected. And that is my worst fear."

"I think my brother realized that too," Eleanor said. "I think Dennis was trying to save Walter from the demon." She shuddered at the thought of Walter encountering an evil spirit. It had scared her half to death, and there was no telling how a boy like Walter might be traumatized by it.

"Can I stay here tonight?" Eleanor asked. "I want to watch Walter again. Can we do it together?"

"If that is your wish," Simon said. "But I won't make the same mistake twice. I will tell you what I told your brother." He took one step closer to her, bringing their faces very close. "You should leave town. Pack up the house and just run away. Whatever is inside is not happy to have people there, and it will harm you, just as it harmed me. It may even do worse things."

Eleanor clenched her teeth. "I hear you and I understand you. But I am staying. I have to finish what my brother started."

Simon Cole nodded his head. "So be it. Do as you must."

18

Eleanor spent the remainder of the evening in the sanctuary. The sun had set and the church grew dark. The lights were on, dimly illuminating the room. She sat alone in the first pew, staring up at the statue of Jesus. His head was cocked to the side, his face portraying many emotions at the same time — pain, despair, and hopelessness. The crown of thorns was upon his head. Blood trickled from his brow and from the holes in his pierced palms.

Eleanor kneaded her hands as she studied the statue, mounted so high above her on the cross. It was so gruesome, so dark.

She wondered if she should pray. But she didn't. She felt a prayer to God right then wouldn't do much. Who was she to live her whole life without Him, and then, just when things in her life seemed the darkest and most confusing, fall at His feet and ask for help? If the roles had been reversed, she would have sent God away.

She laid down on the pew and, despite the cold and

the hard wood, she fell asleep. Until she was shaken awake.

Simon Cole stood over her, his face very close to hers. The church had grown cold. "It is two forty-five in the morning." He checked his watch again, then nodded. "Two forty-six. It is time."

They climbed the narrow stairs. Despite being accustomed to the ascent, Simon still struggled to get up the steps. He used his cane and leaned heavily on the wall to keep his balance. Eleanor stayed several steps below him, giving the old man space.

"I watch from the window here," Simon said. He drew up a chair and sat in it. "Sorry I do not have another."

"It's okay." Eleanor crouched near him and leaned against the table with Simon's notebook. He took out a pen and made note of the date and time. Then, he reached over and turned off the oil lamp, plunging them both into darkness. "I always keep the light out," he said. "I do not want anything to know I am watching."

Anything. Not anyone.

They waited in the darkness. Neither of them spoke. The only sound was the light rustling of an overgrown branch that scraped against the roof of the church.

Movement appeared out of the left side of the windowpane.

Walter.

The boy walked slowly, the same walk he had the night Eleanor had followed him.

He passed through the arch of the graveyard entrance and went to stand in front of Carrie Carson's grave.

Simon picked up his pen and made a note of the time

in his notebook. "Three in the morning exactly," he said, mumbling.

"Why do you track the times?" Eleanor asked.

"To find the pattern," Simon said. "And to take the average. All the times average to three o'clock in the morning."

Eleanor furrowed her brow as she concentrated on Walter. He had come to stand in front of the grave, completely still and straight.

"Should we go down?" Eleanor asked.

"Hmm." Simon groaned. "I think not. We will not tear him from his trance and only invite the evil upon ourselves."

"Is it better to have that evil upon Walter?"

"Of course not." Simon seemed genuinely sad when he spoke. "But what can we do? We must proceed wisely. To rush in is foolish and will only harm ourselves as well as him."

Then, without warning, Walter turned his head. And stared up at them.

"He knows we're here," Eleanor whispered, as if Walter could hear them. "How?"

"He doesn't know," Simon said. "But the demon does."

Walter then slowly raised his hand and pointed at them. The exact same way as he had done the night before.

"It's going to come in here," Eleanor said. "Whatever that thing is. That's what he did last night, and it appeared."

"It cannot come inside the church."

Eleanor remembered him saying that. Were they truly safe inside?

The building began to shake. The walls trembled and the furniture rattled. It was like being in a minor earthquake. Then the tremors ceased.

"What was that?" Eleanor whispered, her voice trembling.

"It does not like us watching," Simon said. "We must be careful."

The church shook again, this time rattling more violently. "Shit!"

"Quick," Simon said. "We need to get to the first floor."

They went down the stairs, much slower than they should have. The building continued to quake as Simon used the wall to lean on to ease himself down the steep steps. The shaking of the building threatened him, and Eleanor thought that at any second, he would tumble down. His body was so fragile that he would break something.

They made it to the first floor. The statue of Jesus shook. The windows rattled in their panes. The lights above swayed back and forth as if something was swinging on them. Cracks formed in the walls and ceiling, bits of plaster raining down onto the floor.

"Come on," Eleanor said, grabbing Simon's free hand and trying to pull him along faster. "We have to get out of here!"

"We cannot go out there," Simon said, "because then we are vulnerable."

"But if we stay in here, the place will cave in around us."

Simon made no move to follow her. She saw a resolve in him, one that meant he would not leave the walls of his church no matter what. It was like a captain going down with his ship.

A piece of the ceiling fell from above, landing just inches away from Eleanor. If it had struck her head, it would have knocked her unconscious.

"It's me," she said. "I'm the one it doesn't like."

Then she turned and ran toward the foyer.

"Eleanor!" she heard Simon shout after her. "Please! Don't go out there!"

Eleanor burst through the doors and out into the cold night. She ran down the front steps and turned to look back at the church. As soon as she was outside, the entire building stopped shaking.

She turned toward the graveyard and looked where Walter had been standing.

The boy was gone.

A loud cracking sound. Then the cross that was mounted on top of the church leaned to the side, snapped off its base, and fell onto the roof. It slid down the tiles and then over the edge, landing heavily with a thud in the grass a few feet from where Eleanor stood.

Seeing the symbol of Jesus lying unceremoniously in the grass, broken and destroyed, gave Eleanor an unsettling feeling.

Then something caught her eye.

Dennis's house. The lights were on inside.

19

She started walking toward it. Then the house began to shake, like the church had.

The lights went on and off. The windows started moving up and down, opening and closing, all at the same time and by themselves. The front door opened and closed, flying open and banging against the wall, slamming shut again.

The whole house had come alive, shaking and moving and shining and falling dark again. It made a tremendous amount of noise.

Eleanor stared in disbelief. It was as if the house was yelling at her, trying to scare her away.

Then it all went quiet again.

And the front door of the house lingered open. As if daring her to enter.

Eleanor wanted to run back to the church, but it would only attack the church again, and the building was too old and would not be able to withstand it.

Slowly, she climbed the steps and entered the dark

house.

Inside was a mess. The furniture had been blown over. All of Dennis's belongings that she had carefully arranged in the living room were scattered. The chairs and sofa had broken legs, the cushions ripped open and white cotton strewn about. Somehow, her suitcase had been thrown downstairs, her clothes tossed everywhere.

The entire place looked like a typhoon had hit.

She reached over and turned on the light, illuminating the vandalism. And then she heard it. A soft creak.

Not on the stairs. Not the sound of someone walking on old floorboards. It was the sound of a door opening. It came from above her, and she knew exactly what it was.

She climbed the stairs, and when she got to the second floor, she turned to the left and peered at the staircase that led to the third floor attic. Up top, the door that was previously locked now stood wide open. There was nothing but darkness on the other side.

Eleanor's throat closed up. Something was inviting her, telling her to come in. She knew she should run away.

Dennis. What did you have up there?

She climbed the wooden steps, again feeling like each one was ready to collapse under foot. She took out her cell phone and turned on the bright flashlight.

This was the room from the story Simon told. The one where the family had supposedly hidden from the mob. It had not worked. They had been discovered and murdered with an axe anyway.

Eleanor stood at the entrance to the room, using her light to scan the contents before actually stepping in.

From where she stood, it only seemed like a storage room for junk. Just like any other attic.

Then she stepped in. Immediately, she felt different. The room was icy cold, and she got the distinct feeling that she was not alone.

She gasped. Her breath frosted on her lips.

Most of the junk in the room had been covered with sheets to keep the dust away. She scanned the ceiling with her white beam, but found no light.

The only thing that had not been covered with a sheet was at the far end of the room. There, in the light of her flashlight, was an easel. Yet another one that had belonged to her brother.

And there was a painting on the easel.

When she approached, and shined the light over the artwork, she saw the familiar image of the graveyard at night. Except this one had two figures. There was Walter, and he was holding hands with a taller shadow.

It was the entity she had seen.

There was a box at the foot of the easel. Inside, Eleanor found five more paintings of the same thing. The graveyard, Walter, and him holding hands with the entity, all almost exact copies of each other.

The final painting in the stack was different. When the light fell on it, Eleanor gasped. It was a closeup of the demon, black and dark and nothing but a shadow. The eyes were two silver holes in the face that pierced through her, even though it was only a picture. She removed it from the box and placed it on the easel.

She heard a squeaky footstep behind her.

She gasped and whirled around, shining her light at the entrance of the attic room — accidentally knocking down the easel. The painting and easel collapsed to the floor, a loud crash echoing through the attic.

She saw no one.

Then another squeak, this time louder. Something was in the house again, on the second floor, and it was heading right toward her.

There was only one way in or out of that third floor attic room, and she couldn't just stay there.

She quietly crept to the open door of the attic room. She held her breath. The icy chill made her shiver.

A step away from the exit, the door swung shut by itself, the force rattling the walls.

And embedded in the back of the door was an axe.

Eleanor let out a shriek at the top of her lungs. Surrounding the axe were the dark remains of blood that dripped from the axe's blade and onto the ground.

The blood was not in a random pattern. It looked as if someone had dipped their fingers in and written a message:

You will die too

She reached for the handle and yanked on the door, but it would not open.

"Help me!" she shouted, banging on the door. "Let me out of here!"

The door rattled on its hinges as she attacked it, but it would not budge.

The space around her filled with sound, soft and barely coherent over her desperate shrieking. It got louder, and Eleanor listened. It was a disembodied voice. Although a breathy whisper, it was very loud, almost as if it was inside her head. She knew it was speaking, but she could not understand the language.

Eleanor backed away from the door, looking around the room for the source of the voice. But there was no one. The speaking seemed to come from everywhere all at once.

"Leave me alone!" she shouted at the emptiness around her.

The voice continued speaking. It sounded as if it were chanting, putting some kind of incantation on her.

She thought the voice was coming from somewhere behind her, and she whirled around and met the eyes of the demon in Dennis's painting, lying face up on the floor where it had fallen. The silver eyes glared at her from the artwork, seeming more alive now than it had before.

The voice grew louder. The jumbled words were more aggressive, angrier. Fear stabbed her chest, her body tensed, looking in every direction, waiting for something to attack her.

She heard splintering wood and turned toward the door, watching in horror as the axe dislodge itself from the bloody mess.

It flew through the air, twirling round and round.

Right toward her.

She dropped to the ground. It whirled by her, lodging itself deep into the wall opposite the door, the handle wobbling.

"Please!" she shouted. "Let me go!"

Then the chanting stopped.

The only sound was her gasping breath. A cold sweat had broken out all over her body, turning to ice against the frigid air in the attic.

Eleanor's eyes darted from side to side, her body frozen in place. She was trapped and she was completely at the mercy of this… thing.

Then, all at once, her body lifted off the floor.

Some incredible force had picked her up, controlling all parts of her body. Her arms floated up, outstretched to her sides. Her legs dangled five feet above the ground. Even her hair stood on end as if she'd been electrocuted.

She was completely frozen, unable to move anything except for her eyes. Captured and held by the invisible entity, like a puppet.

Another noise.

The axe dislodged itself from the wall again, floating over the floor, carried by something invisible, and hovered a few feet in front of her.

This time, it would not miss.

She could not dodge this one.

Another noise on the far end of the wall.

The lock on the attic door broke and the door flew open.

She fell.

Whatever held her let her loose. The axe dropped to the floor, landing with a loud clang. Eleanor's body crumpled and fell five feet onto the hard wooden floor. Her head cracked against the ground, sending a jolt through her brain that made her vision turn black and fill with dots of light.

The world around her was hazy, and she wasn't sure if she lost consciousness. She didn't think she did, but still, her vision was blurry in the dark room.

The familiar face of Simon Cole hovered over her, his eyes concerned. "Miss Eleanor? Are you okay? What happened?"

"The demon," she managed to say.

It almost killed me.

And it had made it look so easy.

20

They passed the rest of the night in the church. The sun rose and brought with it a grey morning.

It took those last few hours of the night for Eleanor to feel normal again. For the dark feelings of dread and despair to dissipate, and for the pain in her head to subside. A big knot had grown on the back of her skull.

Even though her head hit the ground the hardest, her entire body felt achy and fatigued. The demon's touch made her feel like she'd just run miles in the sand.

Her eyes burned with tiredness. Her head spun, replaying what she had just experienced. But all the thoughts were an exhausted blur.

Simon came into the sanctuary, returning from his upstairs bedroom. "How are you feeling?"

"Complicated." Eleanor figured that most accurately described the odd sense of melancholy, desperation, and hopelessness that swarmed inside of her.

Her phone buzzed in her pocket. Odd. Who would text her at sunrise?

When she checked her screen, though, she saw six missed calls, all from Sean, plus three texts from him, all spread out between the hours of the night.

"What?" She hadn't heard her phone ring the night before.

"What's wrong?" Simon asked.

Then Eleanor remembered. Whenever the demon was present, her phone always malfunctioned. "That thing seems to be able to mess up my phone."

"Ah. Yeah." Simon sat on the pew near her. He used his hands to shift his leg into a more comfortable position. "Dennis used to complain about the same thing."

Sean had tried to reach her, but none of it had gone through until just then. She then remembered that she was supposed to call him the evening before when he asked her to not stay at Dennis's house.

"He's probably freaking out," Eleanor said.

She called him back and brought the phone to her ear. It took a long time before the signal connected, then Sean answered, but didn't say anything.

"Hello?" Eleanor asked, figuring the reception was bad. When she checked her screen, though, all five bars were present. "Sean, can you hear me?"

Nothing but silence on the other line. But someone had definitely answered.

"Sean?"

A roar erupted from the phone's speaker, so loud it pained her ear. Eleanor threw the phone and scurried away from it on all fours like a frightened animal. The noise sounded like it came from a beast that was not of this world.

"Miss Eleanor," Simon said, rising quickly from the pew.

Eleanor crawled to the back of the room, underneath the feet of Jesus on the mounted statue above her. The overwhelming emotion from the night before had all come back to her. Tears filled her eyes. She knew that thing was coming over the phone, trying to interfere with her getting help.

Simon bent and picked up the phone.

"Don't," Eleanor said, her voice cracking.

Simon peered at the screen, then slowly brought it to his ear. First he listened, then said, "Hello?" A few seconds passed. "Hi, Sean."

Eleanor let out the ragged breath she'd been holding.

"Yes, she's here with me," Simon said, looking at Eleanor like she was a hurt puppy. "No, she isn't exactly all right. We've… had a long night. Yeah, we're at the church. Sure. See you soon." He hung up the phone. "Sean is coming."

Eleanor nodded and wiped a tear that had fallen down her cheek.

"What did you hear on the phone?" he asked.

"It."

Simon approached her slowly, leaning heavily on his cane. "It seems like it is getting more aggressive."

"I think so," said Eleanor. Her heart had finally started to return to its normal rhythm. She now knew beyond a shadow of a doubt why Dennis had killed himself. If he had endured this creature popping out at him all the time, had experienced the same emotions that it gave her, then she knew that after a certain amount of time, she would also eventually break.

"Come," Simon said, helping her to her feet. "Let's go sit down over here."

Eleanor allowed herself to be escorted to the pew, where she sat, her hands trembling.

Sean arrived twenty minutes later carrying the cross that had once been on the roof of the church. He immediately went to where Eleanor lay on the pew. "Are you okay?"

"I don't know."

"Come on." He took her hands and helped her sit up straight. He appraised her for a few minutes before he looked at Simon. "What happened last night?"

"A lot to explain," Simon said.

"Then maybe start at the beginning."

Eleanor barely listened as Simon recounted the events of the night before. She heard about how Simon had hobbled as quickly as he could on his bum leg to the house, then up the stairs after hearing the commotion, and breaking open the lock with his cane.

She shivered as he told Sean about how he had seen her hovering in the air, and then fall.

He was just in time. That thing was ready to kill me.

Sean looked at Eleanor in disbelief, waiting for her to corroborate. She said nothing.

Sean rubbed his face. He had skipped a day of shaving and his beard had begun to come in. "I always knew there was something funny about that place."

"I don't want you to get involved," Eleanor said weakly. "There is something very terrible going on, and it's dangerous."

"What do you think it is?" Sean asked.

"A demon," Simon told him. "An inhuman spirit that does not belong in this world."

Sean adjusted the cap on his head and glanced toward the statue of Jesus behind him. "How do we get rid of it?"

"I've tried once before," Simon said, his voice low. "And I failed."

"Where did it come from?" Sean asked.

"It is a creature from hell," Simon said. "It has no age. It has always existed."

"Yeah, but why is it just now becoming active?" Sean asked. "Why is it attacking people now?"

Eleanor looked up at the two of them. "It has something to do with Carrie Carson." Simon and Sean looked at her, confused. "That's the grave that Walter stands in front of. Why her?"

"The sheriff's wife?" Sean asked.

"I assume so." Sean and Simon exchanged a glance. Neither of them seemed to know of a connection. "Why else would Walter stand in front of her grave? The demon must have something to do with her. Do you two know anything about her?"

"Well," Simon said. "She passed away about two years ago. Pancreatic cancer, I believe. The sheriff has never been the same since."

"And what is her relationship with Walter?" Eleanor asked.

Simon shrugged. "There is none, as far as I know."

"My mom knew Carrie Carson," Sean said. "They used to meet once a month with some other ladies and play cards."

"What do you know about her?" Eleanor asked him.

"Not much. All I heard was she was a nice and normal woman." Sean furrowed his brow. "But now that you mention it, I remember Mama saying that she started acting weird as her cancer got worse. You know, like it was taking its toll on her. I guess that's normal."

"Weird how?" Eleanor pressed.

"Can't really remember." Sean removed his cap and scratched the back of his head. "Been a few years now."

"Can you ask her?" Eleanor said.

Sean shrugged. "Yeah, I guess so."

"There's a connection somewhere," Eleanor said. "And we need to know what it is."

Sean checked his watch and then took out his phone. "I'll give her a call."

When he stepped away to make the call, Simon walked over to where Eleanor sat on the pew. "This is too much. You've been through a lot. Maybe you should let this rest and then head home as soon as possible."

"Dennis was trying to protect Walter from this thing," Eleanor said. "He failed. I can't leave without finishing what he started. And I'm going to need your help."

Simon looked away. His grip on his cane tightened. "I tried once before."

"Then what? We just leave Walter to continue messing around with the demon? I experienced how this thing can make you feel. Sensed what it wants to do to me. At any point, it could turn around and do that to Walter. We have to protect him. He's been visiting this thing for more than three months now, and if we just stand by and leave him to it, then something horrible will happen."

Simon looked as if he were about to cry. Because that was exactly what he'd been doing — standing by. Ever since his attempt to get rid of the demon with Dennis had failed. Eleanor could see the dilemma in his eyes, could sense his pain. She saw how afraid the old pastor was, and she could not blame him.

"For Walter," she said.

Simon closed his eyes and slowly nodded his head. "For Walter."

Sean returned to them, tightly clutching his phone. He removed his cap and ran a hand through his hair.

"Did she know anything?" Eleanor asked.

"Uh. Yeah." Eleanor and Simon waited for him to speak. Whatever his mother had told him didn't sit well with him. "I think you're on to something, Eleanor."

21

"You're going to exit to the right in a few miles." Eleanor tracked the icon on her phone's GPS, following the highlighted route.

It was eight o'clock in the morning and she and Sean were driving down the highway in his truck.

"You sure about this?" Sean asked.

"It's the only place left to look."

Back at the church, Sean had told them that his mother remembered Carrie Carson's rapid change toward the end of her battle with cancer. She had mentioned several times that she had begun seeing a fortune teller.

"How is a fortune teller going to help someone dying of cancer?" Eleanor had asked.

"That's the thing," Sean had said. "Around here, fortune tellers do more than just predict the future. They're involved in all kinds of dangerous things."

His mother had refused to talk more about it. Like Sean, she was a Christian, and did believe in certain dark things and did not like to talk or think too much about them.

Eleanor had searched on her phone for a fortune teller and found one shop on the very outskirts of Finnick. That had to be the place Carrie Carson was going.

Sean had agreed to take Eleanor out there. She had a feeling that if she could talk to that fortune teller, she would learn something new.

The GPS brought them right to the shop, called Madame Celeste's Magic Shop. It was a small place with a parking lot only big enough for three cars. The store and the surrounding area looked completely deserted.

The sign on the front promised a wide array of wares.

Spells. Potions. Incense. Readings. Tarot Cards. Charms. Occult Books.

Sean groaned. "I don't like it."

"I don't either," Eleanor said. "But this has to be the place she was coming."

The bell above the door jingled when they walked in. The store was ice cold and cluttered beyond belief. Voodoo dolls, some small and others life-size, dangled from hooks in the ceiling. A bookshelf contained large, leather-bound books with pentagrams inscribed on the front. Another shelf had candles, incense, statues, tikis, idols. The counter at the front of the store, a glass case, contained outlandish jewelry that looked as if it had been worn during ancient ritual sacrifices hundreds of years ago.

"Hard to believe a store like this exists around here. Much less stays in business," Eleanor said.

Sean's arms were folded across his chest, as if trying his best not to touch anything. "There's a big voodoo culture down here in the south," he said. "Stores like this can be pretty popular."

A woman stepped through a beaded curtain in the back of the store. She did not seem pleased to see them. "I thought I heard voices. We're closed." She smacked loudly on her gum.

"Sorry," Eleanor said. She assumed this was Madame Celeste. "We won't stay long." She took a step toward the woman. "I was wondering if I could talk to you about something."

The woman checked her watch. "I'll start readings at ten."

"It isn't about my fortune," Eleanor said. "I wanted to ask you about someone who used to come into this shop. At least, I think she used to come here."

"Honey, do you know how many people come through here?"

"Please. It will only take five minutes."

The woman glanced back toward the room she'd come from, a distressed, impatient look on her face. Then she went behind the counter and leaned on her elbows. "What can I do for you?"

"My name is Eleanor Lawson," Eleanor said. "I was hoping to ask you about one of your customers. Carrie Carson."

At the mention of the name, Celeste's body tensed up and she stopped chewing her gum. She slowly straightened and then put her gum in a tissue and threw it away. "I haven't seen her in a long time."

"Two years," Eleanor said. "Sadly, she passed away."

Celeste did not seem put off by the information. "She

had cancer." Her voice was rough from many years of a heavy smoking habit.

"Yes."

"And what does any of this have to do with me?"

Sean cleared his throat and stepped forward. "My mother was friends with Mrs. Carson. She told me that as her cancer got worse, she got more and more strange. And started coming here frequently."

"Yes," Celeste said, shifting her weight from one foot to the other. She did not meet their eyes, only kept glancing back toward the beaded curtain from where she'd came, as if desperate to disappear.

Eleanor studied Madame Celeste, could sense her discomfort with the conversation. "Would you be able to tell us what she came in here for?"

"That was a long time ago now. I don't really remember."

"Please?" Eleanor said, laying her hands on the glass display between her and the fortune teller. "It's important."

Celeste gave Eleanor her full attention for the first time since she'd come in. Looked her up and down, as if trying to decide how much she should say. "Has there been some trouble?" She asked as if she already knew.

"You could say that," Eleanor said.

Celeste took a deep breath and scratched at her wild, untamed black hair. "She was desperate toward the end. I remember that. She became obsessed with continuing to live on, even after she had passed."

"And she wanted you to help with that?"

"I don't know if she even knew what she wanted," Celeste said. "At first, I would read her fortune. I'd tell her what she wanted to hear, that everything was going to be fine and that her cancer would go into remission. But I don't think she believed me. Whatever she had, I think they'd already told her it was incurable and she only had a few months to live. So she became more focused on remaining in this world after she passed, one way or another."

"So what happened next?"

Celeste glowered at her. "I'll tell you the same thing I told Carrie. This is not really stuff to mess around with."

"I understand that," Eleanor said. *You have an entire shop devoted to the occult. How responsible could you be?*

"She wanted practical things she could do to ensure more time here on Earth. She wanted rituals, spells, incantations, anything to make a deal with the other side."

"And you gave it to her?"

"Look," Celeste said. "This is supposed to be a novelty shop. People come here to buy voodoo dolls and spell books just for fun. This isn't serious. Madame Celeste isn't even my real name. I told Carrie this, that I wasn't some expert on the spiritual world, but at that point she wasn't listening. She saw me as her only hope when the doctors had let her down. So what could I do? I gave a book of rituals and she seemed pleased with that because she never came back again."

"Do you remember what book you sold her?" Eleanor asked.

Celeste nodded her head toward the book shelf. "The black one over there. It's pretty popular with the kids."

Eleanor took the book from the shelf and flipped through the pages. There were rituals with specific scripts for summoning entities, pictures on how to set up magic circles, and suggestions for supplies needed to make contact with the other side, such as candles, metals, and incense.

Sean looked at it over her shoulder and shivered when he saw a page filled with pentagrams.

Demon summoning. There was a whole section in the book concerning it.

"I'll take this," Eleanor told Celeste. The fortune teller shrugged and rang her up on the register.

"Have you ever done any of the rituals described in this book?" Eleanor asked as she paid.

"No," Celeste said. "I think it's all made up for fun. Kind of like a gag gift. But even if I did believe, I still wouldn't mess around with it too much. I tell made up fortunes and sell statues and voodoo dolls for money. I don't need anything from the other side."

"What are you going to do with that?" Sean asked when they returned to the truck.

"I'm going to find what Carrie found," Eleanor said. "And whatever she did, maybe there is a way we can undo it."

22

Summoning demons is not something that should be taken lightly. These entities can be very helpful in obtaining wealth, health, and lovers. They can also be useful in causing harm to enemies and adversaries. But remember, there will always be a debt to pay, and the demonic will always collect. Consider very carefully before summoning one of these entities.

Remember. If you call them, they will always come.

What followed was a list of demons and their names. There was also an accompanying rough sketch, detailing creatures that just looked like combinations of animals, such as lions, tigers, bats, and bears.

"This can't be real," Eleanor said, scrutinizing the pictures. "How could one author know what all these demons look like?"

"The lady did say it was a gimmick book," Sean said. He drove while Eleanor rode, the leather-bound tome open in her lap.

Eleanor flipped the page and almost tossed the book

away. There was a full page illustration of tall, human-like shadows, all parts of their body completely black except for their eyes.

"What's wrong?" Sean asked.

"This is it," Eleanor said, turning the book so he could see. Sean only glanced at it for a moment before returning his eyes to the road. "This is what I saw in Dennis's house." *This is what almost killed me.*

Eleanor returned the book to her lap and flipped the page. There were more symbols, incantations, and instructions on how to summon the demons and how to ask them for what you wanted.

The whole thing made her shiver. She imagined Carrie Carson, weak from her cancer, sitting alone with the book and asking otherworldly monsters to give her a longer life.

"Well, look who it is," Sean muttered.

Eleanor looked up just in time to see Walter on his bicycle, heading down the sidewalk in the opposite direction.

"What's he doing out at this time of day?"

"It's Saturday," Sean said.

"Oh." Eleanor twisted in her seat and saw Walter fading smaller into the distance. "Turn around."

"What?"

"Make a U-turn. Let's follow him."

"Follow him? Why?"

"Because Walter is connected to all this somehow, and we still don't know why. Can we see where he goes?"

Sean thought about it, but then made no objection. He slowed the truck and turned around in the middle of the road, then sped up to follow Walter.

The Gravewatcher

They caught up with him as he steered his bicycle onto Main Street. Sean slowed his speed as he tailed the boy, and eventually he jumped the curb onto the sidewalk and leaned his bike against a streetlight. He unfastened his chain and attached it to the pole, checking to make sure it was secure before disappearing inside a nearby general store.

Eleanor and Sean watched from across the street. "I'm going in," she said, removing her seatbelt.

"This is crazy," Sean said. "He's doing normal kid things on the weekend."

"As long as he speaks to a demon in the middle of the night, he isn't doing normal kid things." Eleanor got out of the truck and followed Walter into the general store.

It was freezing inside, with old tiled floors that must have been from the 70s. There were only a few aisles, and the selection of food was slim. Walter spoke with the elderly man behind the register, and Eleanor pretended to browse a shelf as she listened to what they were saying.

"I'm glad you came in," said the man behind the counter. "I haven't seen you in a while."

"I've been busy, Mr. James," Walter said.

That made Mr. James laugh. "I'm sure you have. A very busy boy. And have you been a good boy?"

Walter nodded. Mr. James then said, "Good. I wouldn't expect anything less. That means I have something for you."

Eleanor ventured a peek around the edge of the shelf. Walter stood with his back to her, looking up at Mr. James on the other side of the counter, who beamed at him.

Mr. James bent down and rummaged below the register. "I know it's in here somewhere," he mumbled. "Ah. Here it is." Then he popped back up, holding a small toy, an action figure in plastic wrapping. "You like these, don't you? Do you have this one yet?"

Walter took the toy and held it in both hands, studying it.

Then, in a sudden fit of rage that came from nowhere, Walter threw the toy onto the ground as hard as he could. Both Mr. James and Eleanor jumped, completely startled.

"I have that one already!" Walter shouted.

Mr. James stared at the boy, eyes wide, completely caught off guard by what was happening. Walter jumped onto the toy several times, stomping it into the ground. "I don't want it! I don't *want it!*"

Then he ran from the store.

Mr. James watched him go, astonished.

Eleanor crept out from behind the shelf and Mr. James looked at her. "I don't know what that was about. He's usually such a good boy."

Eleanor picked up the remains of the toy and handed it over the counter. "You mean he's never done that before?"

"Never," said the old man. "What's gotten into him? I hope everything's okay at home."

Through the window, Eleanor watched as Walter unfastened his bike chain and peddled off furiously.

She returned to Sean's truck. "Did Walter have a long shopping list?"

"The weirdest thing," Eleanor said. "The guy in there tried to give him a toy and Walter just freaked out and threw it on the ground and started stomping on it."

Sean's face wrinkled. "What? That doesn't sound like him."

"Come on. Let's keep following him."

Sean started the engine and set out to catch up with Walter further down Main Street. "I don't know what you're hoping to find by doing this."

"At this point, I'll take anything. Any little clue."

Walter's next stop was a place called Jimmy's Pizza. He was very methodical about locking his bike to the streetlight pole. Then, he disappeared inside the restaurant.

"Jimmy's," Sean said. "Best pizza in town."

Walter went inside, then came back out a few minutes later and sat down at one of the outside tables. A few minutes later, a man, presumably Jimmy, brought out a small pizza and placed it in front of Walter.

"Is that Jimmy?" Eleanor asked.

"Yeah. But the restaurant is named after his dad, whose name is also Jimmy. That Jimmy right there went to high school with me."

Walter did not seem pleased. He frowned at the pizza, then looked up at Jimmy. They spoke, and Jimmy explained something.

"What's going on?" Sean asked. "You don't send back pizza at Jimmy's."

Then Walter flew into another rage. He shot up from the table and knocked the pizza onto the ground. Jimmy jumped out of the way just in time, otherwise it would have gone all over his pants and shoes.

"Whoa," Sean said.

"That's it," Eleanor said. "That's how he freaked out in the grocery store earlier."

Walter stormed off, leaving Jimmy scratching his head

as he watched the boy go. Walter unlocked his bicycle from the streetlight and tore off down the road.

"Okay, that is a little weird," Sean said. "I've never known Walter to do anything like that."

"Something's up," Eleanor said. "People say he's apparently such a good boy, but today he isn't. Keep going."

They accelerated up the road. As they passed, Jimmy began the messy process of cleaning up his patio.

Walter's next stop was the park.

The boy peddled his bicycle up the gravel road to the playground and dropped it on its side by the swing set. He sat down in the center swing and slowly rocked himself back and forth.

Sean inched his truck forward and turned into the parking lot behind the playground. They were far enough away that Walter either did not notice their presence or simply chose to ignore them. The three of them were the only ones in the park, and Walter kept his back to them.

"What are we going to do now?" Sean muttered as they watched. "Sit here and wait for him to go somewhere else?"

Eleanor chewed her lip. There didn't seem to be much point in idling in the parking lot and waiting on Walter. "I'm going to go talk to him."

"And what? Ask him why he's being so mean to everyone?"

Eleanor wasn't quite sure what she was going to say to him. The two last times they had spoken, he'd shouted at her with the voice of a demon and then, the next day, lied straight to her face. "Come with me, Sean. Maybe he'll be more open with you."

"I don't really know him all that well."

The Gravewatcher

"Please. We have to do something. He's connected to this somehow and maybe now that he's alone, he'll actually tell me the truth."

Sean watched her for a long time. She could tell that he realized she wasn't going to let up until they did something, and he was right. "Fine." He killed the engine, and they climbed out of the truck.

They crossed the open field of the park toward the swing set. Walter still had not noticed their approach.

Then another car appeared in the distance. It pulled into the other gravel parking lot on the opposite side of the park.

"Shit!" Eleanor whispered.

It was a police cruiser.

23

"What?" Sean whispered back.

Eleanor grabbed his arm and pulled him behind the bathroom building that was nearby the playground, and they hid around the corner. "Carson's here."

"Why?"

Eleanor peeked around the corner. Tony Carson emerged from the police cruiser and slowly ambled over to where Walter sat on the swing. As he went, he looked around the deserted park in all directions, making sure they were alone.

"Afternoon, Walter," Carson said. Eleanor's hiding place behind the bathroom building was close enough to make out what he said. "Aren't you going to say hello to your friend Tony?"

"Hi, Tony," Walter said. He rested his head against the swing's chain.

Carson struggled to lower his huge body onto the ground in front of the swing set. Once he was down, he was just below eye level with Walter. He removed his hat. "We haven't met in a long time."

Walter didn't respond. He did not seem pleased to see Carson. Eleanor could not see his face, but she could sense that he was afraid.

What the hell is going on? Why do Carson and Walter meet up in secret?

"Do you have anything you want to share with me?" Carson said. "Since we haven't seen each other in a while, I'm sure you have a lot of new information."

"I have a bad feeling about this," Sean murmured in Eleanor's ear.

"She wants you to know that she is okay," Walter said. "She knows she's told you this before, but you still worry and she doesn't want you to worry. There is no pain anymore. There is peace. And she is happy that she still gets to be with you and watch over you."

Tony Carson did not say anything for a long time. He only quietly digested what he heard, his eyes glued to the ground.

And then his shoulders bobbed up and down as he began to cry.

Walter only sat on the swing and watched the sheriff have his moment. Loud sobs of anguished pain erupted from his large frame.

"She knows you don't sleep at night anymore, and that you stay up and walk around the house, watch television, and drink, and that none of it helps you sleep. She says you need to stay off the sleep medicine and try to exercise more. That will help you. Also that you've gained a lot of weight since she passed, and she doesn't like to see you neglecting your health. She wanted me to remind you how you were when the two of you met. You were very strong and athletic. Do you remember?"

Carson continued to sob as he listened.

"She knows you're still very angry at what happened, but that you need to let it go, eventually. She understands why you can't, but it would make her happier if you chose to move on. You can't continue like this."

Carson blubbered into his hands like a baby, and Eleanor was surprised to see such emotion come from the man who had once been so hard toward her.

His wife. He thinks Carrie is communicating to him through Walter.

Eleanor saw a broken man, one who had not weathered the storm of Carrie's death well. Her heart hurt for him, even though it did not excuse the way he tried to get rid of her. She now understood, in a way, why he did it.

"Unreal," Sean whispered as he watched next to Eleanor.

After a few minutes, Carson got his crying under control. He wiped his red, puffy eyes and looked back at Walter. "Sorry to do this in front of you, Walter. You're a good boy, and you're really doing an amazing thing for your friend Tony. You have a great gift, and I'm glad you get to share it with me."

"There's more," Walter said.

Carson smiled. "Okay."

"You lost your lucky pocket knife last week, didn't you?" Walter asked. Carson nodded. "It's between the couch cushions. Carrie knows you usually sit in the recliner, and she says you forgot that you sat on the couch one day last week to tie your shoe. That's when it slipped

The Gravewatcher

out and fell between the cushions. If you look there, you'll find it."

"Oh," Carson said. "Yeah, you're right. I've been looking everything for that dang thing. Next time you talk to her, tell you I said thank you."

"I will," Walter said.

Carson fought to stand back up. He brushed the dirt from his uniform trousers. "Do you want a ride home, Walter? It's the least I can do to thank you for helping me with this. We can put your bike in the trunk if you want. I'll even let you play with the siren."

"There's another thing I forgot," Walter said. "Carrie told me to tell you that it was very important."

Carson frowned. Even seemed a bit nervous. "I'm listening."

"There's a woman," Walter said. "I don't know her name, but Carrie said that you would know. She is in town and she shouldn't be. She said you need to take care of her. I tried to ask her what she meant because I was confused, but she wouldn't tell me anything else. She said that you would understand."

A strong glower came over Carson's face. The emotional side of him had gone and Eleanor recognized the grim, stubborn sheriff she had interacted with.

Sean and Eleanor exchanged a glance.

"Is that so?" Carson asked.

Walter nodded.

Carson tucked his thumbs behind his belt and hiked up his pants around his substantial gut. "It just so happens that I do know what she's talking about. And you're right, Walter. It is very important. I'm glad you told me. Thank you."

"You're welcome."

"I'll make sure to take care of this little problem as soon as I can. Now come on. Let's get you home. I'm sure Gretta is wondering where you are."

Carson lifted Walter's bicycle into the trunk of his police cruiser and they drove off together.

"That was the creepiest thing I've ever seen," Sean said once they were gone.

"Not me," Eleanor said. She wiped her sweaty palms on her pants. "But it is still terrible. Carson is using him. He doesn't realize how dangerous this could be."

And the demon also used Walter to warn him about me.

It would only be a matter of time before Carson came for her. There were only so many places to hide in a small town.

"Come on," she said. "Let's get back to the church. I need to talk to Simon."

24

Eleanor and Sean returned to the church in the late afternoon. Dark grey storm clouds had blown in overhead, darkening the sky. Thunder rolled in the distance.

They found Simon in his office adjoined to the sanctuary, sitting at his desk with his glasses on, focusing on the papers in front of him. He removed his glasses when they came in.

"Carrie Carson was seeing a fortune teller," Eleanor said. She dropped the heavy leather-bound book on Simon's desk. He returned his glasses to the bridge of his nose and started flipping through the pages. "But she wasn't much interested in the future. She wanted to find a way to live on, even after she passed away."

Simon glanced at her from atop the lenses, then continued flipping through the book. The images and words seemed to pain him.

"This is dark stuff," Simon said. "No one should dabble in this material."

"Carrie Carson bought that very book. That was the last time the fortune teller ever saw her."

Simon paused when he came to the page that had the pictures of the dark shadow creatures with glowing eyes. He studied it for a few seconds, then slammed the book closed on his desk.

"That is what I saw in the house," Eleanor said. "What Dennis and I both saw."

"It seems she was looking for life after death," Simon said. "But what she found instead was a demonic entity."

"And now it is still around while she is gone." Eleanor said, and Simon nodded. "There is something else. When we were driving home, we spotted Walter on his bicycle." She told him the story about following him around town and then how, ultimately, he had stopped and spoken with Tony Carson.

"He delivered him messages that he claimed were from his wife," Eleanor said.

"God help us all," Simon muttered, leaning back in his office chair. His face wrinkled into a very concerned, fearful look. "It seems Tony Carson thinks Walter is giving him messages from his late wife. That is not the case. It is this demon pretending to be Carrie Carson."

"Pretending?"

"The demonic's main desire is to deceive," Simon explained. "They can do this in a number of ways. They can appear as people they are not. They can perfectly mimic the voices of people, both living and dead. They know languages that have long ago died out because they have knowledge of all the events of history. As you know, they can manipulate our devices and technology and cause them to fail. All of this they can use to lie to us and to frighten us. To make us weak so that they can take over."

Eleanor and Sean exchanged a glance. He looked very uncomfortable with the conversation.

"So what does this mean?" Eleanor asked Simon.

The old pastor leaned forward. "I assume the demon wants Walter, and pretending to be Carrie Carson is the best way of keeping him."

"And then when I interfere, it attacks me," Eleanor said.

"Yes. You threaten to expose its lies. That is why it has come after you. That is why it went after Dennis."

And it is why Simon never leaves the church, Eleanor thought.

"We have to save this boy," Eleanor said. "Walter is acting like this because the demon is starting to get to him. Starting to affect him."

"Yes," Simon said. "And soon it will own him."

"Own him how?" Eleanor asked, knowing she could not bear the answer.

"Once the will is broken, then the demon is free to do what it wants," Simon said. "Walter's heart and mind have been pried open after all this time. Soon he will be possessed."

Eleanor swallowed. "And once that happens?"

"Then he is at the demon's complete mercy. If the demon wants him to kill, then he will kill. If it wants him to kill himself, then he will. The goal is death and destruction only. To cause as much hurt and pain as possible."

"That's horrible," Eleanor said.

Simon stood from his chair and went to the cabinet near his desk. He took from it a small bottle filled with water. "This is the last bit of holy water I have. I used the rest of it when your brother and I tried to banish the demon the first time."

"Are you ready to fight again?" Eleanor asked.

He stared down at the bottle, shifting it back and forth in his hands.

"Simon," Eleanor said, taking a step toward the old man. "What happened the last time you tried to get rid of the demon with my brother? Why didn't it work?"

Simon was quiet for a long time. Finally, he cleared his throat. "Do you believe in God, Miss Lawson?"

"Um." Eleanor swallowed. "Maybe? I don't know. I guess. My parents used to bring us to church when we were younger."

"I asked you if you believe in God."

Eleanor shrugged. "I suppose I've always thought there was something out there. Bigger than myself who could have made all this." But the theory of evolution in college science classes had made a lot of sense to her, too. "Maybe I do now," she continued, her voice quiet. "After seeing this demon. If this thing exists, then anything could exist. Right?"

Simon nodded. "And faith. Believing in God is not enough. Do you have faith that He is who He says He is, and that He will do what He promises He will do?"

Now Simon was getting deeper and Eleanor wasn't quite sure how to respond.

"I lost faith, Miss Lawson," Simon said, his voice cracking. "The older I've grown, the more I begin to think that maybe we are all alone here. Then I catch myself with these crazy thoughts and try to kick them away. I'll tell myself that after a few more sermons on Sunday, I will be back to my old self again. But no. I've been slipping further and further into disbelief as time goes on."

Tears formed around the rims of Simon's eyes. Eleanor glanced at Sean, who also looked heartbroken as he watched the old pastor confess.

"When your brother came and told me what was happening to him, I knew I had to be strong. I knew I had to *believe* that God would banish this demon if we asked Him to in His name. But instead of finding my faith again, all I could wonder was how God could create such a despicable creature and allow it to turn His creation into its playthings. And so no matter what I did, no matter how hard I prayed or what I said, that thing got the best of me. They can see inside you, you know. They know what you are thinking, and even worse, they know what you are feeling. This thing knew I didn't believe the words I was praying, so it was able to toss me around like I weighed nothing. Broke my leg and broke my faith at the same time. And when Dennis had nowhere left to turn, he took his own life. And it's all because of me."

Simon broke down, burying his face in his hands. Eleanor moved to comfort the man, putting her arm around his shoulders. She let him cry there for a few minutes, allowing him to get everything off his chest.

"Dennis doesn't blame you," she said. "No one in this town could possibly face what you did and come out the same on the other side." She already knew she wouldn't. "The best we can do now is fight this thing for Walter. That was who Dennis was fighting for, anyway. Just because he is gone does not mean this is over. We can do this, but we all need your help."

Simon's sobs slowed. Eleanor felt the wetness through

her shirt. He lifted his head again, drying his eyes with the back of his hand.

"I will do this for the boy. Because I know that he is running out of time. But I am afraid that I will not be strong enough. I am old and weak, and this thing has a power that we will never fully understand." He held the bottle out to Eleanor. "Here. You will need this before I will. It has marked you as a target. This can protect you."

Eleanor took the bottle from the pastor. It looked to be nothing more than water. "What do I do with it?"

"It is a weapon of God," Simon said. "Throw it at the demon when it appears. Call upon God's name and command it to leave. It must obey whatever you tell it to do if you command in the name of the Lord. And have faith He is listening."

Eleanor slid the small bottle into her pocket. The thought of coming face to face with the demon again made her feel sick to her stomach. "They really don't like God, do they?"

"God is their enemy. They will do anything to mock Him and blaspheme Him in any way possible. That is why it calls Walter to him at three in the morning."

"Why three?" Eleanor asked.

"To mock the Holy Trinity," Simon said. "Three in the morning is a time of darkness, the opposite of three in the afternoon, a time of light. It is also why many of the things demons do usually come in sets of three."

Eleanor shuddered. She'd also been woken up at three in the morning two nights before, when the demon had appeared in the house. Now she knew it had *wanted* her awake.

And I found out about Dennis three months after he died.

"What do we do now?" she asked.

"First," Simon said. "We prepare. When facing the demonic, we must spend time with God and ready ourselves." He returned to his chair. "And for me, that means finishing tomorrow's sermon. Can I expect the two of you in church tomorrow?"

"Yes," Eleanor said.

"Good. That is the best place to be in times like these."

Eleanor and Sean left the pastor alone in his office to finish his work.

"Why don't you come stay with me for the night?" Sean said. "For real this time."

"Of course," Eleanor said. After the night before, there was no way she was spending the night in Dennis's old home again.

But she wondered if her location mattered. Would the demon come for her even if she wasn't staying in the old house? Was being so close to Sean putting him in danger?

"Are you sure?" she asked. "I'm a little cursed at the moment."

"Positive," he said, and they went out to his truck.

25

Sean lived alone in a simple three-bedroom home in a neighborhood where all the houses looked the same. It was sparsely but neatly furnished with a large leather couch, a big screen television, and framed posters of sports teams. A true bachelor pad, but one that belonged to a man who was somewhat on his feet.

"Nice place," Eleanor said when they went in through the back door and turned on the light.

"Thanks. Bought it last year."

"What do you do for work?" she asked.

"Accounting," he said.

"Oh." Eleanor was surprised, although she didn't know why. Perhaps she took Sean for more of a blue-collar worker.

"Yeah. Kind of a numbers nerd. Always have been. I'll show you your room."

Eleanor could tell the guest bedroom didn't get a lot of use, but regardless, the double bed was made and ready and the attached bathroom was stocked with the basics.

He brought her some of his clothes — athletic shorts and a t-shirt. He'd agreed to supply her with everything since she had no desire to go back inside Dennis's house for any of her clothes — not even for a minute. All she'd brought with her was her purse.

"Will this be all right?" Sean asked, showing her the clothes.

"Yes, they're perfect."

"Okay." He laid the clothes on the end of the bed. "My room's this one just down the hall. Come knock if you need anything."

"Thank you," she said.

As soon as she closed the door, her eyelids grew heavy and her body seemed to lose all desire to even stand. It had been so long since she'd slept, and being inside a real house that finally felt safe was very relaxing.

She found towels and soap and shampoo in the bathroom. After her shower, she opened one of the toothbrushes and tubes of toothpaste Sean had put on the bathroom counter. When she crawled into bed, she found the mattress and pillows surprisingly soft, and before long, she drifted off to sleep.

Only to be awoken by the shrill alarm clock on her phone.

Eleanor stirred awake, her eyes trained to open as soon as that unique noise filled the room. She rolled over to stop the alarm clock, and then realized.

I didn't set my alarm.

She glanced at her phone just in time to see the time tick over from 2:59 to 3:00. She sat up straight in bed, suddenly wide awake.

Oh no.

The room was dark and very cold. Eleanor didn't remember it being that chilly when she went to sleep, but now she shivered despite the warm blanket covering her body.

Then her phone started buzzing. Someone was calling. The phone screen lit up the dark bedroom.

She slowly turned the screen toward her.

Dennis.

She gasped and pushed the phone away from her, scurrying out of the bed as if it were suddenly filled with bugs.

The phone continued buzzing, even long after her voicemail should have picked up.

"Go away," she whispered.

She remembered what Simon had told her. Demonic entities could manipulate her devices — manipulate anything, really — could bend reality, and would, just to scare her and weaken her. She shuddered to think about what she would hear on the other end of the phone if she answered.

It's trying to bait me. Thinks I will answer if I think it's him. But I won't fall for it.

She stood against the wall, watching the phone buzz from afar until it finally stopped.

"Eleanor."

She whirled around. The voice had come from behind her.

Dennis's voice.

It had been a long time since she'd last seen him or heard him, but she'd recognize it anywhere. It had come from the guest bedroom closet that was right behind her. Now she pressed her back against the opposite wall.

Did I imagine that?

Tap-tap-tap. Like a single finger knocking against the other side of the door.

"Eleanor."

She let out a squeal that she stifled with her hand over her mouth. Tears sprung from her eyes.

It can mimic voices. It isn't him.

But how had that thing followed her to Sean's house?

"Eleanor, please open the door."

Tap-tap-tap.

She turned and fled from the guest bedroom, down the hall and into the dark living room, where she sharply stubbed her toe on a chair.

"Ow!"

She hobbled around, grabbing her foot and collapsing on the couch. Her toe throbbed, and she wondered if she'd broken it.

Then came the pounds on the front door.

Bam-bam-bam.

Not knocks. It sounded as if someone angry on the other side was demanding to be let in. Eleanor forgot the pain in her toe all at once.

Bam-bam-bam.

Louder that time. Stronger. The door actually rattled on its hinges.

The light in the living room turned on. Sean stood at the end of the hallway, standing in his boxer shorts and t-shirt, alarmed. "What's going on?"

Unable to speak, Eleanor pointed toward the door, her hand trembling.

Sean slowly started walking toward it. "It sounds like they're trying to bring the house down."

Bam-bam-bam.

Sean moved quickly toward the door. "Sean, don't!"

But it was too late. He threw it open and wide and turned on the porch lights. No one was there.

Eleanor let out a slow, ragged breath, her heart pounding. Sean stuck his head out the door and looked both ways, then closed the door when he found nothing.

Bam-bam-bam.

This time from the back door. Sean ran toward it and threw it open, but again, there was nothing there.

"What the hell is going on?"

"It's here," Eleanor said. "It's trying to scare us."

"You mean…"

"Yes. Everything is in threes. And it mimicked Dennis's voice in the guest room closet, trying to scare me."

Sean closed the back door and joined her on the couch. They sat still and quiet, looking around the room, waiting for the next disturbance to come.

Eleanor knew that neither of them were going to sleep for the rest of the night. It was getting what it wanted. Not letting up, not allowing them to rest or have a moment's peace. Eleanor could see that if this had happened to Dennis over the course of several months how he would have eventually broken.

"It's getting more active," Eleanor said. "It knows that we want to fight it. It's trying to attack us first."

She couldn't wait for the sun to come back up and to return to the old church, where she knew it was safe.

26

The rain came down all through the sermon.

Eleanor could not remember the last time she'd been to a church service. Her parents had made them go as a family when she was very young, but that had not lasted long. Once Dad had quit, her brothers had made the argument that they shouldn't have to go if Dad didn't. Eventually, Mom quit pushing the issue, and from then on, church had never been a part of her life.

Now, she sat in the same pew as Dennis had, right where Simon had told her Dennis's favorite spot had been. Simon Cole stood on the stage wearing his dark black robe, Bible open on the podium. There was no microphone, but the booming storm outside did little to drown out his surprisingly powerful voice.

"It was pride that made Lucifer believe that he was equal to God," Simon said. "And it was for that pride that God cast him out of Heaven and into Hell. All the angels that aligned themselves with Lucifer were also cast out, and these fallen angels have been the enemies of us and God since the beginning of time."

The sermon was sparsely attended. Eleanor supposed it was the rain that kept people from leaving their houses. Still, the faithful had come, and she wondered if Simon's message had been inspired by recent, unfortunate events.

"These demons still prowl the Earth," Simon went on, meeting eyes with each attendee as he scanned the room. "They wait for us to become weak, to falter in our faith. Only then can they attach to us, influence us, and lead us into temptation and sin. And if we give in, then we will also be cast from Heaven, just as they were. This is their desire. This is their purpose. They were separated from God for eternity, and now their only mission is to see us suffer the same fate."

Eleanor wrung her hands in her lap. She glanced to her left, where a familiar woman sat in a maroon dress. The sermon was half finished before Eleanor had spotted Gretta Washington sitting across the aisle. She was alone, and her attention was completely focused on Simon Cole.

After a few final hymns, the service ended right at noon, and afterwards Simon Cole stood by the church's front door to greet the guests as they left. Eleanor hung behind and then approached him last. "Very timely message, Pastor."

"Unfortunately," he muttered. Then he tilted his head toward the graveyard behind the church. Gretta Washington walked among the headstones. "She visits her husband every Sunday," Simon said.

Eleanor took a deep breath. "I'm going to go speak to her."

It was a risk. She assumed Gretta had been the one to inform Sheriff Carson that she had gone to visit her trailer, and that had prompted him to try to force her to leave town. If she told him that she was still around, then no doubt Carson would return.

Eleanor hung by the entry archway of the cemetery as she gave Gretta some time alone with her husband. She'd stopped in front of a headstone in the center of the field, looking down, appearing oddly similar to her adopted son whenever he made his nightly visits.

Then, after a few minutes, Eleanor went to her. The tall, unkempt grass was wet against her legs and her feet sank in the sloshy mud and rain water.

When she went to stand next to her, Gretta did not acknowledge her. Instead, she never broke her gaze from the headstone.

ALBERT WASHINGTON

Finally, Gretta spoke. "He's been gone for ten years. There isn't a day that goes by that I don't miss him."

Odd. Eleanor had been expecting a more tense conversation, given the icy conclusion of her last visit.

"I'm sorry to hear that," Eleanor said.

Gretta shrugged. "That's life, I suppose. Eventually, it ends. As you well know because of poor Dennis."

Then she turned to face her, and Eleanor gasped. She had a black eye and a bandaged cut above her eyebrow. Her bottom lip was swollen.

"Oh my God," Eleanor said. "Who did this to you?"

Gretta tried to keep it together, but she broke and began to cry.

Eleanor stepped forward and hugged the woman,

forgetting about the last time they'd encountered each other. Gretta cried into her shoulder for a few minutes before getting control of herself.

"I'm sorry," she said, wiping her eyes. "I'm just so afraid."

"Afraid of what?"

"Afraid for my Walter."

Eleanor studied her as she took a tissue from her purse and wiped her eyes. She winced when she touched the bruised one.

"Walter did this to you?" Eleanor asked.

"I don't understand what's come over him lately," Eleanor said. "He's always been such a good boy."

Eleanor remembered the temper tantrums he'd thrown when she and Sean had followed him around town the day before.

"Gretta," Eleanor said. "Why did Walter do this to you?"

"I don't know," Gretta said. "He has been very irritable and he is quite strong for his age."

Eleanor took a step toward Gretta. "I know what's going on. And I want to help. My brother Dennis wanted to help."

Gretta held her gaze for a long time. Eleanor could sense the other woman was trying to make a decision.

"I don't care what happens to me anymore," Gretta said slowly, carefully enunciating every word. "I need your help. Please save my boy."

"If you knew what was happening, then why lie to me the first time that I came?"

"Because of him."

"Tony Carson."

The Gravewatcher

Gretta nodded.

"Did he threaten you?"

"I don't know why Walter was chosen," Gretta said. "But that didn't matter to Sheriff Carson. He told me I was to let Walter do what he must. If anyone interfered, including me, then there would be trouble."

Eleanor's fist clenched at her side. "I'm so sorry. I wish I'd known."

"If I told you, then he would have done much worse to me." She pointed to her face. "I thought everything would be fine. Walter was never hurt. But now he is changing. And I thought it was just some harmless ghost. I've always believed they've existed, but I never thought such a thing would ever be a part of my life."

"Gretta." Eleanor put a comforting hand on the woman's arm. "Walter has not been talking to a ghost. It is something else, something far more dangerous. I've seen it and I've felt it, and my brother did too. Walter isn't changing, but this thing is causing him to act this way." Gretta's eyes widened, and she looked like she was going to cry again. Eleanor hated to frighten the poor woman, but there were things she had to know. "Dennis was trying to help your son, but this entity got the best of him. But it won't happen to me. Whatever it takes, I will make sure Walter is freed."

The woman enveloped Eleanor into a tight hug. "Thank you," she whispered. "What do you need me to do?"

"Nothing," Eleanor said. "Just wait for tonight. Let Walter come. And when he does, I will be waiting for him."

And she would be. Interfering with his little ritual

meant the demon would attack. And when it came, she was sure to be ready.

27

After church was over and the congregation had all gone home, Eleanor and Sean lingered behind in the church. The storm had fallen silent for the moment, leaving behind only a grey sky and chilled air. Water dripped from the tree branches and the ground was soaked and muddy.

"I presume you will be waiting around for Walter tonight," Simon said.

"Yes," Eleanor said. "It has to be tonight. I feel we are running out of time."

Simon nodded slowly. Eleanor had told him about the demon terrorizing them at Sean's house the night before. As a result, neither of them had slept after it had woken them up. The lack of sleep was starting to compound in Eleanor, but she knew there would be no rest until everything was resolved.

"In that case," Simon said, "I need to spend some time in prayer."

The old pastor slinked to the back of the sanctuary and climbed the steps up to his bedroom.

Sean waited until he was gone before speaking. "What's the plan?"

"I'm not sure," Eleanor said. "All I know is that Walter can't be allowed to talk to that thing anymore. After that, it will probably come for me." She idly played with the cross necklace around her throat, the one Sean had given her.

"Are you afraid?" Sean asked.

"Terrified." She already knew firsthand how dangerous it could be. "I need to get some air."

She stepped out of the church foyer and into the cool afternoon. She pulled her jacket tight around her as she sat on the front steps of the church, studying the graveyard and Dennis's house nearby.

Her phone buzzed in her pocket. It startled her greatly after what her phone had done the night before. But when she checked the screen, she saw it was her brother Carl calling.

"Carl," she said, answering quickly.

"Eleanor," he said. "How are you?"

"Not well," she said, her voice low and tired.

"What's going on?" He asked, although he did not sound too concerned. In fact, he sounded wooden and hollow.

"You're never going to believe me if I told you. Not in a million years."

"Tell me." His voice was flat and emotionless.

"No, really. I'm going to have to tell you some other time, after it's all over. Because it's so crazy that —"

"Don't worry about it then," Carl said. "It doesn't matter, anyway."

Eleanor frowned. "What do you mean?"

"You should just give up."

"Give up? Carl, what are you talking —"

"You should have left when you had the chance but now it's too late and I'm going to send you to hell just like your brother *you stupid fucking bitch there is nowhere to run God can't save you because he hates you* —"

The phone went hot in Eleanor's hand and she dropped it to the ground. It landed face up where the display was a garbled mess of glitchy static. Then the screen went black.

Eleanor's breaths were sharp gasps as the panic set in. She stood with a hand on her chest, trying to calm herself.

After she got herself under control, she went down the front porch steps and picked up the phone. It had cooled off, and when she pushed the power button, it turned back on without a problem.

No more answering phone calls, she told herself. The demon could mimic *any* voice it needed to in order to catch her off guard.

When she looked up, something caught her eye in Dennis's house. A figure stood in the bedroom window, staring at her.

She was too far away, so the figure was featureless. It had the appearance of a very tall and slim man — the same shape as the shadow she had seen a few nights before.

Eleanor froze. The figure in the window did not move either. She slowly stepped backwards, stumbling on the church's porch steps as she did. Then she went back inside.

It can't come inside the church. Simon's words came back to her as she rushed into the sanctuary. As soon as she'd stepped out for some air, the demon was quick to remind her that it was near.

And in order to fight it — in order to save Walter — she would eventually have to leave the safe, holy walls.

———

Later that night, the storms threatened to return. Thunder boomed in the distance, strong and loud, shaking the flimsy walls of the church. Eleanor, Simon, and Sean were huddled in the sanctuary, peering out the window. Water from the rainstorm before still beaded on the window.

"Two fifty-six," Simon said, glancing at his watch. He'd spent the afternoon alone, upstairs in his room, praying and reading the Bible.

Eleanor's hands began to tremble. She knew the demon was out there waiting for her. Gretta Washington's tear-streaked face came back to mind, and her desperation and fear.

Dennis. I'll finish what you started.

"I'll bring him inside," Eleanor told them.

"And then?" Sean asked.

"Then I don't know," Eleanor said. There was no predicting what the demon would do once its victim was taken away.

There was movement in the dark distance.

"There he is," Simon said.

The Gravewatcher

Eleanor took a deep breath and released it slowly, steadying herself, although knowing there was nothing she could do to truly prepare.

She pushed open the doors of the church. It was the first time she'd gone outside since she'd seen the figure in the bedroom window. Her eyes couldn't help but look in that direction now. Dennis's house was a dark shadow against the night sky.

Walter approached her as if in a sleepwalking trance. He moved slowly toward her, eyes open but not seeing her. When he was near, she crouched down to his level and put her hands on his shoulders, and he stopped.

"Walter," she said gently.

The boy broke out of his trance, blinked several times and, for the first time, seemed to really see her.

"Are you there?" Eleanor whispered.

"Yeah," he said.

Their eyes locked onto each other and held for a long time. To her left, she heard Sean come out onto the front porch of the church.

And then Walter's body started to tremble under her hands. "Help me."

He sounded so desperate, so hurt, so afraid. Tears came to Eleanor's eyes. "I will. I promise."

Walter began to cry.

Eleanor took him into her arms, embracing him like her own child. Walter hugged her back.

She crouched there and let him cry while she rubbed and patted his back. "I've got you. I won't let anyone hurt you." She hoped she could keep that promise.

When Walter stepped back and looked at her, his face

was red, his eyes wet and puffy. He wiped his nose with the back of his arm and sniffed. "I'm so afraid."

"I know you are," Eleanor said. She glanced to her left. Sean and Simon watched, both looking very sad and tense.

I am too.

"Come on," she told Walter. "Let's go inside the church. It's safe in there."

She straightened and took his hand in her own. As they went, Eleanor got the strong impression that she was being watched from afar. But when she looked, nothing was there. At least, nothing she could see.

It's here.

And it would not be happy to see Walter disappear inside the church.

28

Walter went immediately to one of the center pews and sat down with thighs together, hunched over, arms folded across his stomach. He was shivering.

Simon went over to him. He sat in the pew in front of the boy and twisted his torso to face him. "Walter. I've been praying for you."

"You shouldn't," Walter said.

"Why is that?"

"There's no point."

Eleanor joined them and sat down next to Walter. "We are here to help you. We were all waiting for you outside because we knew you would come."

Walter turned away from the floor and looked her in the eyes. Their faces were very close, and Eleanor could see his tears. "Thank you for coming. I didn't think you would."

"What do you mean?"

"Dennis said you would be the one to come."

Eleanor's breath caught in her throat. "You sent me the message." Walter nodded. "Of course I came. My brother was trying to help you, wasn't he?"

"I don't remember much," Walter said. "My memory… There are big parts that just… aren't there."

Eleanor glanced at Simon. The pastor nodded. "That is not your fault, Walter. These things are normal when coming in contact with…"

"Don't worry, Walter," Eleanor said, putting her hand on his. "I'm here to finish what Dennis started."

"You can't," Walter said. "You should leave. There's nothing you can do."

"That isn't true," Eleanor said, although she wished she believed it more. "You're safe inside the church. There is nothing in here that can hurt you."

"It doesn't matter," Walter said. "It will get me, eventually. It wants to take me because it thinks I'm stupid. It tells me I have a disease and I'm broken and it's the only thing that can help me."

"Oh, Walter," Eleanor said. "None of that is true."

"It's a liar," Simon said. "That is the only thing a creature like this knows how to do. Lie to us and try to scare us."

"Maybe I should just go out there," Walter said. "If I go, then it will leave us alone. If I don't, then it will come looking for me, and it will be mad."

"No," Eleanor said. "You can't go out there."

"But I have to," Walter said. "You don't understand."

"And you never will understand." The loud, familiar voice came from the front of the church, startling Eleanor. Even Sean, who was still standing in the aisle between the pews, had not seen him come in.

Sheriff Tony Carson stood there, glaring at them. Eleanor stood. Simon did the same, leaning heavily on his cane.

"Sheriff," Sean said.

But Carson held up a hand to silence him. He never took his eyes off of Eleanor. "I thought I told you to leave."

"How can I leave when I know what you're doing to this boy?" Eleanor shot back.

"Sheriff," Simon said, his voice calm and steady. "Let's sit down and talk about this."

"We're not talking about anything."

"Listen to me, please," Eleanor said. "I'm very, very sorry about what happened to Carrie."

Carson winced. "Don't say her name."

"What happened was very unfair, and no one deserves that. But Tony. It isn't your wife who is speaking to Walter."

"Shut up!" He turned away from her, as if the words physically pained him.

And Eleanor realized that somewhere deep down, Tony Carson must have considered the possibility that it was not his wife. But it didn't matter. Just the hope that it *was* her was enough to bring him comfort, to lessen the pain of her death.

"This monster is trying to harm everyone," Eleanor said. "Especially Walter. And you're allowing it to happen because it's tricking you."

"Stop!" Carson shouted at her.

"Sheriff," Simon said. "There are some very serious spiritual and supernatural things at work here. We need to put an end to this madness before we all lose our lives."

"Stop saying that!" He was shouting now.

"Sheriff, please," Sean said, and he took a step toward Carson.

And Carson took his pistol from his belt and aimed it at Sean's chest. Everyone froze.

"I'm disappointed in you, Sean," Carson said. "You were always Carrie's favorite student in Sunday School back in the day. And who tossed that football with you when your dad ran off?"

Sean lifted his hands in the air. "I understand, sir. But all of us are trying to help you."

"Enough." Carson's words were biting and hard. "Walter. Go outside into that graveyard where you belong."

Walter looked back and forth between Carson and Eleanor, but the one with the gun was always in control. He slid out of the pew and walked out of the church.

"You can't mess around with this," Carson said, speaking to Eleanor now. He aimed his gun at her. "Carrie did those wacky rituals inside that old house over there. Said it was haunted and the most likely place to connect with the other side. Well, she did, but I wouldn't know about it until two years later when Walter started playing around in there. Carrie was able to speak through him after that. I guess her spirit was hanging around the house since it's where she did her magic."

"Tony, it isn't —"

"Then your brother moved in. Got involved with Walter and tried to mess up everything Carrie had planned when she was alive. So he got what was coming to him."

Eleanor saw the crazed look in his eyes, a hunger to maintain control no matter the cost.

"What do you mean?"

"Dennis did not kill himself," Carson said. "He got in the way and threatened my connection with my wife's spirit. So I stepped in and took care of it." Eleanor felt the world fall out from underneath her. "I tried to make you leave town, but you refused. Now I'll have to handle you the same way I did him."

Carson pulled the hammer back on his pistol.

"Watch out!" Sean shouted, and pointed toward the foyer.

Carson turned, and in that split second, Sean rushed him, grabbing Carson's gun arm and forcing it down. The gun went off, the shot echoing off the walls of the old church. Eleanor screamed and covered her ears.

The two men went down together, tumbling and wrestling, each trying to gain control of the gun.

"Eleanor!" Sean shouted through gritted teeth as he struggled. "Get Walter!"

Eleanor ran past them and noticed a blooming blood stain spreading on Sean's white shirt, at his stomach.

He's hit!

But he fought so ferociously, and Eleanor wondered if he even knew he'd been shot. There was only a certain amount of time before he grew weak and couldn't fight anymore. Then Carson would finish him off.

She found Walter standing near Carrie Carson's grave. She ran over and scooped him up in her arms and threw him over her shoulder like a sack of potatoes, surprised at his weight but driven by adrenaline.

She ran away from the graveyard, toward the road, not sure how long she could manage to keep the boy hoisted onto her shoulder.

Then she hit a wall.

It felt quite literally like she'd run into one, but there was nothing there. Just an invisible force field. She stumbled backwards, confused.

Then something swept her feet from under her and she landed face first in the cold, tall grass. Walter fell on top of her.

At first she thought Carson had caught up with her, but when she looked around, she saw nothing and no one. And she understood.

"Help me," Walter said, frightened.

A split second later, his body was dragged toward the cemetery, unseen hands pulling him through the grass.

Walter screamed and extended his arms, desperately looking to Eleanor for help. She chased after him, then dove, grasping his fingers and pulling back against the invisible force. The boy's face was filled with agony at the pain of being pulled in two different directions.

"Let him go!" Eleanor shouted. The air all around her felt heavy and dark, confirming its presence.

"It's hurting me!" Walter shouted.

Then the thing let go. Eleanor and Walter fell back together.

"Come on," Eleanor said, getting to her feet, breathless, not wanting to waste any time. "We have to get out of here."

Walter nodded and stood with her, ready to go. But then the demon took her instead. Eleanor was lifted off her feet and into the air.

"Put her down!" Walter shouted, pulling at her leg, trying to yank her along, but he was not strong enough.

"Run, Walter!" Eleanor managed to say. Moving her

mouth took tremendous effort, fighting against the demon's hold on her body. "Run away!"

Walter looked at her for a few seconds. Guilt marred his face.

"Go! Now!"

He turned and ran. Right toward the house.

29

No! Not there!

He soon disappeared into the old home.

He probably thought he could hide there. But Eleanor knew it was the worst place he could have gone.

And she was powerless to go after him. She levitated above the ground in the middle of the field, completely at the mercy of the demon. All she could do was wait for it to decide what to do with her.

A booming voice came from the front of the church. "In the name of the Lord Jesus Christ, I command you to let her go!"

And then she fell. She landed on the ground, completely limp, jolted by the impact. She looked over at the church and saw Simon Cole standing there, his arm extended. In his hand, he clasped a wooden cross.

She had no idea his voice could be that powerful. But it had worked. The entity had to obey commands made in the name of God. It was powerless in the face of the Lord.

"Eleanor!" Simon called to her. "The house!"

Eleanor was on her feet a second later. She sprinted toward the old house, hoping it wasn't too late to get to Walter.

When she got there, the entire place was just as she'd left it. Dark, quiet, still, and a complete mess from when the demon had thrown the furniture everywhere.

"Walter!" she shouted. She found the boy standing on the stairway, on the middle step, looking down at her.

"Walter, come here," she beckoned. "We have to leave!" Her rental car was right out front. They could get in there and drive away.

Another voice came from upstairs. From the third floor attic.

"Walter. Come here, honey." It was the unmistakable voice of Gretta Washington.

Walter looked up, his eyes filled with hope and relief.

It can mimic voices.

"Walter, no!"

The boy was already sprinting up the stairs. Eleanor followed, taking them two, three steps at a time. She tripped at the end, stumbled, and fought back to her feet.

Walter bounded up the wooden steps to the third floor, where the attic door remained wide open. He ran inside the dark room, and the door slammed shut by itself. Eleanor landed hard against the door, trying the knob, but it was locked from the other side.

She pounded on the wood. "Walter! Come out of there!"

Silence.

Shit!

She pounded on the door again, trying to force it

open. Simon had gotten it open when she'd been trapped inside. Surely she could do the same.

The demon had Walter right where it wanted. Eleanor felt tears come to her eyes. The sting of failure and defeat.

The silence of the house was broken.

Downstairs, the front door slammed, followed by heavy footsteps in the foyer.

"Eleanor," Carson called for her, low and slow and taunting. "I know you're in here."

Eleanor cupped a hand over her mouth. She wanted to cry or scream. But she knew she had to be completely quiet.

Heavy boots clomped on the wooden floor on the first story, Carson stalking slowly into the living room, and then the kitchen. She imagined his gun outstretched, ready to fire.

"You can come out now," Carson called. "Dennis also tried to hide, and you know what happened to him."

Then she heard him ascending the stairs.

She crept slowly down the steps that led to the third floor attic, hoping the creaking under her feet was not loud enough to be heard. She closed the door to the second floor landing, blocking her from view.

She waited, pressing her ear against the door, tracking Carson's slow steps as he ascended to the second floor.

If he checked the bedroom first, then his back would be toward her. If she was quick enough, she could jump him and hopefully wrestle the gun from his hand.

She heard Carson stop at the top of the stairs. He stood still, probably trying to decide which room to look into first.

Then another sound came from behind her. The squealing of the attic door opening.

Eleanor turned slowly. And almost screamed at what she saw.

Walter. Standing at the top of the steps in the doorway. His eyes glowing white, identical to those of the demon. In his hand, he held the bloodied axe from the night before.

Possession. What Simon had told her the demon wanted all along.

Then Walter started walking toward her.

"Walter!" she tried to whisper as loud as she dared.

But it was not Walter in there. Those white, glowing eyes made that abundantly clear. The demon had finally taken him.

It slowly closed the gap between them, one step at a time.

"I know about that attic on the third floor," Carson called out. "That's where Dennis tried to hide, you know."

Carson on one end, the demon on the other. Each closing in on her.

When Walter was in range, he rose the axe high above his head, his face blank and unknowing, the bright eyes piercing in to her.

He swung, and the only way Eleanor could dodge was to fall through the door and onto the second floor landing.

Where she landed right at the feet of Sheriff Carson, his gun outstretched.

30

Carson's eyes glanced quickly from Eleanor to Walter once he realized she was not alone. Recognition changed to confusion when he saw the glowing eyes. "Walter?"

But Walter only rose his axe again and Eleanor rolled away just in time as the axe imbedded itself in the wooden floor with incredible force. Carson also had to jump back to keep the blade from sinking through the toe of his boot.

"What the hell?" Carson shouted, moving backwards away from Walter, trying to keep his gun trained on Eleanor, but was too distracted by what he was seeing from the boy.

Walter ripped the axe from where it was stuck in the floor, then effortlessly stalked toward Eleanor, one step at a time, ignoring Carson's presence.

"Walter?" Carson asked. His gun hand dropped to his side.

"He's been possessed by the demon!" Eleanor shouted

at him.

"Walter, put down the axe," Carson said, ignoring Eleanor.

Walter was within range again. This time he swung the axe sideways, forcing Eleanor to leap backwards. He followed it up with another wide swing, catching just the front of her shirt. It ripped a long gash in the fabric near the neckline.

"Walter!" Not knowing what else to do, Carson raised his gun at the boy.

Although Walter and the demon were not looking at Carson — his back was to him — the thing froze, seemed to sense that it was being threatened. Maybe not it, but the body it inhabited was now in the direct line of danger.

And it didn't like that.

It slowly turned, Eleanor forgotten, and put Carson in its sight.

Carson's gun trembled.

"What the hell is going on?" Carson said.

Then Walter started to walk toward Carson, axe ready.

"Walter! Put it down!"

He isn't going to shoot him.

When Walter was close enough, he swung the axe just enough to clip the edge of Carson's gun, sending it clattering away into the darkness.

Walter grabbed a fistful of Carson's shirt, right at the belly, wrenched, and dragged the big man along with him. Carson used both his hands to try to pry Walter's hand away, but he was unmovable.

Walter tossed the sheriff down the stairs. The big man hit each step hard, causing the entire house to tremble under his tremendous weight. Finally, he came to rest at the foot of the stairs, groaning in pain.

Walter rounded on Eleanor. She dodged the axe again, her breath running short. There was no way she could dance away forever.

The demon buried the axe in the wall again, and Eleanor took the chance to maneuver around and run down the stairs, leaping over Carson's body at the end. She felt a strong hand around her ankle, holding her in place. Carson had her in his iron grip, glaring at her from where he lay on the floor.

"Let me go!" she shouted.

"What did you do to him?" Carson demanded.

"This was your fault!"

Walter started down the stairs, white eyes locked on Eleanor.

Carson pulled Eleanor's leg, his vice grip bringing her entire body to him as if she was in the grasp of a giant snake that was ready to eat her. Next, he grabbed her wrist, and then he got his huge hand around her throat and squeezed. Eleanor felt her breath cut off. She grabbed his wrist and tried to break away, but he was strong as a boar.

"Carson, dear, don't do that."

The voice came from Walter — a woman's voice.

Carson gasped. His hands fell away from Eleanor's throat and she scrambled away.

Walter stood one step above where Carson lay, and was now looking down at him.

"What was that?" Carson said, his gaze meeting the glowing eyes.

"I said don't do that. You know how your temper is

and you need to get it under control." The woman's voice came from Walter without his mouth moving.

"Carrie?" Carson asked. His lip trembled.

"You don't need to worry about me," said the voice. "I am just fine. You just need to worry about you. And stop being so stubborn all the time."

Carson forced himself to sit up. "What is this? Where is my wife?"

And then the voice started to laugh. "You do not get to tell me what to do." Still the voice of Carson's wife, but it was the words of the demon that possessed Walter. "And now the boy belongs to me."

Carson looked at Eleanor, and all at once, understanding seemed to dawn on his face. That this thing he'd been communicating with through Walter was not his wife.

Carson didn't see Walter raise the axe high above his head. Eleanor looked away just as she heard the sickening sound of it coming down, the blade driving into the back of the sheriff's skull.

She forced herself to open her eyes. Walter ripped the weapon from Carson's head, and the man lay still at the foot of the stairs.

The bright eyes found her again and the boy slowly began to stalk.

She backed away slowly, walking deeper and deeper into the living room. Soon, her back would be against the far wall with nowhere left to go.

"Please," Eleanor said.

But the demon had what it wanted — Walter. And now all it had to do was dispatch her.

Near the foot of the couch, she spotted her can of

pepper spray from the other night. She picked it up and sprayed it toward Walter. The stream of fluid hit him square in the face, but did nothing to stop his advance. He didn't even blink.

Eleanor tossed the can at Walter and it clanked off his head, doing nothing to faze him.

The rip in her shirt revealed the necklace she wore around her neck. The one Sean had given her.

She yanked the cord and snapped it. And held the cross at arm's length in front of her, as she had seen Simon do when he had commanded the demon earlier.

Walter stopped walking toward her.

"In the name of Jesus Christ, I command you to leave." She tried, although her voice trembled.

Walter recoiled as if he'd been stung by a bee. But the entity didn't go anywhere. The eyes were still that of the demon. But this time, Walter showed emotion for the first time since the demon had possessed him — fury.

"Leave Walter alone! God commands it!"

Eleanor felt strange invoking the name of God when she never had before in her life.

Then Simon Cole appeared at the other end of the living room, limping heavily with his cane. He still carried the cross that he'd had before. It had taken him that long to cross the field.

"In the name of Jesus Christ, leave this place!" His voice was a lot louder and more commanding.

The demon reacted instantly. It whirled around, furious, and threw the axe at the old pastor.

"No!" Eleanor shouted.

It flew through the air, blade over handle, faster than a bullet. Simon dodged and fell to the side, landing hard on the ground. The axe buried itself in the wall, narrowly missing him.

He scrambled to grab his cross.

The demon was now focused on Simon. It sprinted to him, moving inhumanly fast, grabbed his body, and launched him at the ceiling. Simon cried out upon impact, and then went limp as he crashed back down to the floor.

Eleanor ran over to Simon, terrified at the impossible strength the demon had. Blood leaked from his mouth and there was a nasty wound on his head. His arm was twisted at a grotesque angle.

He looked at her, struggling to move, but all his body did was tremble. But he had enough energy left to say, "You have to believe. You have to have faith."

Walter neared them, the demon glaring at them through his bright eyes, ready to finish them both off.

Eleanor stood. She waited until Walter was close enough and then rammed the cross onto Walter's forehead.

The boy screamed. Except, what came from his mouth was the otherworldly voice, dark and evil. Smoke billowed from the place the cross touched him and hissed like water landing on a hot stove.

She placed the cross on the boy's cheek, and it sizzled just the same, causing the demon to cry out even more.

"In the name of Jesus Christ, I command you to leave this place and never return!"

Walter fell down, weak and powerless. But his eyes were still white. So Eleanor touched the cross to his other cheek, and his entire body started to convulse. "In the name of Jesus Christ, I command you to leave this place and never return!" This time, she said it more forcefully.

She knew in her heart that if something this evil, this demonic, could exist, then that meant there was a God who could defeat it. Who could control it, tame it, and send it back to whatever hell it had come from. And she knew that if God had a plan, then it was His plan for her to come to Finnick to finish what her brother started, and to redeem Simon Cole from his faithlessness.

She withdrew the bottle of holy water from her pocket and removed the cap.

"For the last time," Eleanor commanded, "in the name of Jesus Christ, I command you to leave this place and *never return!*"

Eleanor cast the water onto Walter's body and he reacted as if it were lava. An earsplitting scream erupted from the boy's throat, one of pain, frustration, and defeat.

Then Walter's body stopped shaking and finally lay still. The bright white of his eyes faded out. And Eleanor felt a weight lift from her — from the room and the air around her — and disappear. She felt as if the world before had been tilted, and now was set straight again.

And the entire house was quiet once again.

31

Walter was unconscious but breathing. Eleanor rushed back to the church to check on Sean. She found him in the sanctuary, propped up against a pew, his head hanging limply onto his chest.

"Oh my God," Eleanor said, running to him. When she fell to her knees next to him, Sean looked up at her, dazed. His eyes were only half open. His face was ghostly white and his breath came in short, sharp gasps.

"I'll call an ambulance," she said.

She dialed 911, and they said they would send one right away.

"Send more than one," she said.

"Excuse me?"

"There are a lot of hurt people here." She hung up.

"Walter?" Sean asked, his voice raspy and weak.

"Everything is fine," Eleanor said, touching Sean's cheek. It was ice cold. "Don't worry."

"And Carson?"

"Shh. Don't talk. Help is on the way."

Within ten minutes, three police cruisers that looked exactly like Carson's had arrived. The ambulance was at the church a minute after the cops.

Eleanor rushed them inside, where the paramedics immediately put Sean on a stretcher and carried him away.

"Will he be all right?" she tried to ask one of the guys in scrubs, but they only told her that they had to get him to the hospital as soon as possible.

Eleanor guided the next team of paramedics and police to the old house. They all froze when they saw Carson's body at the foot of the stairs, a pool of blood surrounding him.

"Tony?" The officer's eyes were wide as his flashlight shone on him. He wore the exact same uniform as Carson.

"Over here," Eleanor said, leading them to Walter. They checked his breathing and pulse, which were fine, but loaded him onto a stretcher and rushed him to the hospital, anyway.

"Just what the hell happened here?" asked the police officer. His name tag read Jones.

"It's a long story," Eleanor said. "But basically, Carson attacked all three of us. He shot Sean, and he tried to shoot me and Walter."

Jones put his hands on his hips. "You're going to have to come down to the station."

―――

The Gravewatcher

Eleanor cooperated with the police. She rode in the back of the cruiser with Jones and, when they arrived at the station on Main Street, told him only a slightly altered version of what had happened that night.

She left out all mention of the demon and the supernatural. She told him that she had come to Finnick to collect Dennis's things, was threatened and harassed by Carson when she did, and then told them that he showed up at the house, crazy and unhinged, then confessed to killing Dennis and wanted to kill them too.

"I don't know," Eleanor said. "I guess he figured I was onto him, even though I wasn't."

She told him how she and Walter had run to the house to escape after he shot Sean, where they hid, and then she managed to surprise him with the axe.

"Walter was so afraid he passed out," she explained.

Jones listened intently to her story, his brow furrowed.

Finally, he set down his pen and took a sip of coffee. "The sheriff hasn't been the same since Carrie died. Did you know his wife had passed?" Eleanor did not respond. "He's taken two leaves of absence in the past year, both for mental health concerns. We told him to see someone, but he refused."

"I see."

Jones took a deep breath. "He's been prone to fits of rage here in the office. Especially toward me." Eleanor had learned that Jones was second in command to Carson. "I don't know. His mind and his heart were broken. He must have been paranoid that you found out."

"I guess so," Eleanor said.

"I imagine if I talk to Sean Benson and Pastor Simon about all this, they'll tell me the same thing?"

Eleanor nodded.

Jones closed his notebook and sat back in his chair, rubbing his sleepy eyes. "What in the world was Gretta Washington's boy doing with you three?"

"He and Dennis were close. He came over to the house soon after I came to town."

"You mean you were staying in that old haunted place all this time?" Jones looked at her with wide eyes and shivered.

"Don't be silly, Mr. Jones. Those are just ghost stories."

ELEANOR PARKED her rental car in front of the familiar red trailer. Gretta opened the screen door and greeted her as she walked up.

"Are you all right?" Gretta asked.

"I'm doing better," Eleanor said. "How is…"

"He's getting better every day," Gretta said, looking concerned. "At first, he was very tired all the time, but now he seems to be getting back to his old self."

"Has he been lashing out?"

"No, thank God. It seems all that is over with." The bruises and cuts on Gretta's face had started to fade.

Walter came from one of the back rooms of the trailer and into the kitchen. He only spared Eleanor a short glance before walking down the hallway and into his room.

"Not much to say," Eleanor said.

"He probably doesn't remember you."

Eleanor looked at the older woman. "What?"

"I tried to talk to Walter about everything that happened the other night. But he doesn't seem to remember."

"Really?"

Gretta nodded. "And thank the Lord. The things that he's been through the past three months. No child should ever have to endure that." She began to choke up, and she placed a hand on her chest. "It's my fault. Who would have ever allowed that to happen?"

Eleanor hugged the woman. "It isn't your fault. You did the best you could when Tony Carson threatened you. You didn't have a choice. He was a big bully and it was the only way he knew how to handle the situation."

Gretta Washington sniffed. "I suppose you're right. But still. He's my boy and I should have done more to protect him. I guess I figured if Tony hurt me, then there wouldn't be anyone left to care for him."

"We don't have to worry about that now," Eleanor said. "It's all over. That spirit is gone, and now Walter can go back to being a normal kid."

Gretta nodded, drying her eyes. "We can only pray. Do you want some coffee?"

Eleanor didn't, but accepted anyway.

"What will you do now?" Gretta asked as she served them both a steaming mug.

"I'll go back to New York City. Back to my normal life, and just try to…"

Forget everything that happened here. But she knew that would be impossible.

Although she didn't finish her sentence, Gretta knew what she had been about to say. "No need to ever come back to Finnick, I don't think. You did the right thing while you were here and it caused you a lot of trouble. Best to just try to move on."

"Yeah." Eleanor sipped her coffee.

"How is Simon?"

"I was going to visit him after I left here," Eleanor said. "I just wanted to check on Walter first."

Gretta smiled. "Thank you. What you and your brother did for my boy... I can never repay. You saved him when I couldn't. I can only thank God for the two of you. Your brother gave his life for Walter, much like Jesus gave His life for us."

Eleanor thought that was a bit of an overstatement, but allowed the other woman to take comfort in the idea, anyway. "I'm glad we were here to help."

When she left ten minutes later, Gretta wrapped her in a tight hug. The older woman was stronger than she thought she would have been. "Give Simon my best. Tell him I hope he returns to preaching soon."

"I will," Eleanor said.

ELEANOR DROVE DOWN THE HIGHWAY, following the directions on her GPS. It brought her reliably to St. Benedict Hospital.

It was a small place, just perfect for servicing the small community in and around Finnick. The waiting room was manned by only a nurse and a security guard who were chatting with each other when she came in. A football game was on the television mounted to the ceiling, but there was no one else around to watch it.

As Eleanor approached, the nurse turned to her and gave her a wide smile. "Good morning. How can I help you?"

"I'm here to visit Simon Cole," Eleanor told her.

The nurse nodded and checked her clipboard. She found it quickly and told her that Simon was on the third floor, in room 311.

The security guard took her identification and wrote her first name on a sticker, which Eleanor placed on her shirt.

The old pastor was in bed. His face was bandaged and bruised and a thick, white blanket was pulled up just underneath his chin.

As if sensing her, his eyelids fluttered open weakly, searched the room, then found her. When he recognized who she was, he smiled.

"How are you feeling?" Eleanor asked him.

"Blessed."

Eleanor pulled up a chair beside the bed. As she did, Simon's hand appeared from underneath the blanket, fingers and palm spread, waiting for her. She took his hand. It was warm.

"Are you going home?" he asked her. His voice was croaky from not having been used in a while. Eleanor hoped people were visiting him. Surely Sean was.

"Yes. I am on the way to the airport now."

"Good. Home is where you belong. You've spent more than enough time here."

"I've spent just the amount of time I needed to," she said. She squeezed his hand. "Thank you for everything you did to help me and my brother. And Walter."

"You are the one who saved Walter," Simon told her. "You were strong when my faith was not."

Eleanor smiled.

"But promise me something," Simon said.

"Yes. Anything."

"When you get home, don't keep going as you were. Call your family and get them together. It is important. It can all be taken away so fast."

"You're right," Eleanor said. "And I will. I promise."

And she intended to keep that promise.

Simon Cole readjusted himself in the bed, wincing in pain as he did. "How is Sean?"

"Spoke with him on the phone earlier," Eleanor said. "He told me he's good as new, but I think he's exaggerating. Either way, he's fine."

Sean had also been brought to St. Benedict, where the bullet in his gut had been removed and his wound bandaged. Luckily, it had not hit any internal organs.

Eleanor checked her watch. She only had an hour and a half until her flight.

"Go," Simon told her. "And never come back." He smiled again.

Eleanor chuckled. "I'll try my best."

She kissed him on the forehead before she left. The image of the man tucked into the blankets, suffering from injuries he sustained trying to save her and Walter, would stay with her for the rest of her life.

When Eleanor arrived back in New York, she returned to work the next day. She received many condolences from her coworkers about the loss in her family, to which she nodded, smiled, and said nothing more. They were all confused as to why she'd come back so soon, and her manager even offered to give her more time off. She politely declined.

"More time off is the last thing I need," she told him.

He looked at her, worried. "Okay. But if you change your mind, please tell me."

"I will. Thank you."

That evening, after she'd gotten back to her apartment, Sean called her. "Hey. Just checking to see if you made it back all right."

"I did. How's your stomach?"

"Still hurts, but I'm getting around." He chuckled. "Listen, they rushed Simon into surgery last night, unexpectedly. He's in recovery now."

Eleanor's knees gave out, and she fell onto the couch. "What happened? Will he be okay?"

"They told me he was complaining of more pain, and when they did tests, they found internal bleeding. The doctor told me that he's expecting him to bounce back."

"Oh my goodness." Tears came to her eyes.

"I was with him earlier," Sean said. "He was reading his Bible and was very much at peace. He assured me that because of everything that happened, he's truly found his faith again."

Eleanor took a great deal of comfort from that.

They spoke for a little while longer, and when they hung up, Eleanor spent a long time in silence, reflecting on Simon and the time she had spent in Finnick. Then she whispered a soft prayer to God to protect him and heal him. It was the first time she'd prayed in a long, long time. Hopefully, it would not be long before he was preaching again.

Then she picked up her phone and called her brother.

The Christmas holidays were coming up in a few weeks. Maybe it was time they all got together.

<<<<>>>>

NEVER MISS A NEW RELEASE AND GET A FREE NOVELLA!

My novella Nanny is FREE and exclusively available to members of my Reader Group.

Go to my website to sign up and download your free ebook today! You'll also be notified when I release new books.

www.rockwellscott.com

ALSO BY ROCKWELL SCOTT

The Tenth Ward

Meet Randolph Casey—university professor by day, demonologist, ghost hunter, and paranormal investigator by night. And he's about to take on his most dangerous assignment.

Rand has seen better days—his ex is getting remarried, and a persistent "non-believing" university auditor is threatening his job. The last thing Rand needs is to take on a new ghost hunting case. But when a desperate couple approaches him about their terminally-ill daughter, Georgia, who claims a ghost is visiting her hospital room at night, he can't seem to turn them away.

Rand figures that banishing Georgia's ghostly intruder will be a routine matter. All he needs to do is guide the lingering ghost to the afterlife. But when the ghost returns with a vengeance, attacking Georgia and terrorizing other hospital wards, Rand realizes this is no benign spirit, but an evil demonic entity. He's faced such monsters before, but never one so complex, so aggressive and violent. If he doesn't unravel its ancient origins and discover how to banish it back to hell, a hospital full of people will fall victim to its destructive agenda.

The Tenth Ward is a supernatural horror thriller for readers who love stories about hauntings and battles with the demonic—the truest form of evil that exists in our world.

ALSO BY ROCKWELL SCOTT

A Haunting in Rose Grove

A malevolent entity. A violent haunting. A house with a bloody history. Jake Nolan left it all behind, but now he must return.

Jake has it all — a new home, an amazing girlfriend, and nearing a promotion at work. Best of all, he feels he's finally moved on from the horrors of his traumatic past. But when he learns that his estranged brother, Trevor, has moved back into their haunted childhood home, Jake knows his past is not quite finished with him yet.

Jake rushes to the old house in Rose Grove — a small town with a tragic history — to pull his brother from that dangerous place.

But it's too late. There, he finds Trevor trying to make contact with the spirit that tormented them years ago.

And Trevor refuses to leave. He is determined to cleanse the house and remove the entity. But the supernatural activity becomes too much to handle, and Jake knows they are both unprepared for the fight. Worse, the entity targets Daniel, Jake's young nephew, and wants to bring him harm. And when the intelligent haunting shows signs of demonic infestation, Jake realizes they aren't dealing with a mere ghost.

Jake attributes the evil spirit for driving his parents to an early grave. Now it wants to claim the rest of the family, and the only way Jake and Trevor will survive is to send the entity back to hell.

A Haunting in Rose Grove is a supernatural horror novel for readers who love stories about haunted houses and battles with the demonic — the truest form of evil that exists in our world.

A NOTE FROM ROCKWELL

Hey there.

I would like to thank you for spending your valuable time reading my book. I sincerely hope you enjoyed it.

As you may know, reviews are one of the biggest things readers can do to support their favorite authors. They help get the word out and convince potential readers to take a chance on me.

I would like to ask that you consider leaving a review. I would be very grateful, and of course, it is always valuable to me to hear what my readers think of my work.

Thank you in advance to everyone who chooses to do so, and I hope to see you back in my pages soon.

Sincerely,

- Rockwell

ABOUT THE AUTHOR

Rockwell Scott is an author of supernatural horror fiction.

When not writing, he can be found working out, enjoying beer and whiskey with friends, and traveling internationally.

Feel free to get in touch!

Instagram
https://www.instagram.com/rockwellscottauthor/

Facebook
www.facebook.com/rockwellscottauthor

Twitter
@rockwell_scott

www.rockwellscott.com

rockwellscottauthor@gmail.com

Printed in Great Britain
by Amazon